NAVAHO SISTER

BOOKS BY EVELYN SIBLEY LAMPMAN

NAVAHO SISTER

EVELYN SIBLEY LAMPMAN

Illustrated by Paul Lantz

Doubleday & Company, Inc., Garden City, New York

NAVAHO SISTER

CHAPTER ONE

"Ya-et-eeh," said Mrs. Yucca, stopping on the trail to smile a greeting. "You, too, go to the trader's for supplies?" Her arms were filled with cans, coffee, tomatoes, and lard. Grace, her younger daughter, carried a sack of flour.

"No," said Grandmother courteously. "Today we seek no supplies. Only words."

"Oh," said Mrs. Yucca slowly, her eyes growing thoughtful. Then she added quickly, as though an idea had just come to her, "Tomorrow my husband plans to kill a sheep. Perhaps some fresh mutton would taste good to you. If you will send your granddaughter to our hogan when the sun is so high, I will have some ready for her to bring home."

"Thank you," said Grandmother promptly. "You are generous."

Sad Girl, catching Grace Yucca's eyes upon her, hung her head in embarrassment. Grace Yucca was smiling a grown-up-girl smile, for Grace was sixteen and had been away two years at the white man's boarding school for Navahos. She meant it to be friendly, but Sad Girl read only pity in it.

7

Sad Girl hated pity. Hated and resented it. For all of her twelve years she had known little else. It wasn't that she minded being poor. Lots of Navahos were as poor in worldly goods as she and Grandmother. So long as they had a few sheep which could be sheared and the wool spun into yarn which in turn could be exchanged for flour and lard and a little coffee, it was enough. Occasionally there was a wild rabbit to vary the diet. In good seasons, there were piñon nuts to gather. Many Navahos had no more, and it was not for this that people like Grace Yucca and her mother looked at Sad Girl with pitying eyes.

It was because she and Grandmother had no family, no clan. There were only the two of them. Grandmother's husband and daughters had, one after another, been carried away by sickness. Her only son who, people whispered, must not have been much account anyway, had disappeared, and no one knew where he was. Grandmother's own parents and sisters had been dead many years, and there were no nieces, nephews, or cousins. To be without a family was very sad indeed. It was something no one could help, so everyone felt very sorry and pity showed in their eyes. That was why she was called Sad Girl. It was not her real name, of course. It was a nickname and was never used directly when people spoke to her. But they used it when speaking of her, for it was a quality or trait which was all her own, just as some individuals were referred to as Flat Nose, or Tall Boy, or

Scar Face.

"Does that one," asked Grandmother, glancing at Grace but speaking to Mrs. Yucca, "return soon to the white man's school?"

"She does," nodded Mrs. Yucca proudly. "In twice four days' time she must be ready to make the journey. Our son also."

"What has she learned," demanded Grandmother curiously, "besides to cut off her hair?"

"All the girls at school cut off their hair that way," explained Mrs. Yucca defensively. "It is the way they all wear it. The style."

"It is easier to take care of." Grace nodded. "At the school I have learned to speak English. I can read in their books and write so that others can read what I have set down. And I can sew with a needle and thread and on a machine that pulls the thread in and out of the material. I can cook on the white man's stove, and I've learned about health and sanitation, and I know geography—which tells all about this country and the things in it."

"What good will it do her?" asked Grandmother of Mrs. Yucca. Her voice was earnest, as though she wanted very much to know the answer to the question. "You have no machine to pull thread in and out of material, no stove like the white man uses. Why should she know about health when we have hand-tremblers to tell us what causes sickness and singers to make that sickness well? I know as much about this country as anyone else. I was born here. Why should she learn those things of the whites?"

Mrs. Yucca looked troubled, and Grace answered for her mother.

"Everything is changing," she said. "There is not enough good land on the reservation for all the young people to make a living. There is not enough grass for all of them to own sheep. Many of them must find jobs in other places. We do not know how to find jobs off the reservation or the customs of people who live in towns away from here. Even if we stay here we must learn some of the ways of the white people. Our young men who came back from helping with the war made a name for themselves. They lived with the whites, and many of the white customs they found good. Not all, but some. They want to keep the best of ours and take the best of the white man's ways. It is the same with us who go to school. How can we choose what is best for us if we stay to ourselves and never find out by anyone else?"

Sad Girl lifted her eyes to glance quickly at Grandmother. The old woman was listening carefully, her head nodding slightly. When she spoke her voice was determined, as though Grace had put words to her own thoughts.

"You are right," she agreed. "The world is changing. Our people are changing. In my time I have seen it happen. My granddaughter will see even more changes. I do not know what the white man has to teach, but it is well to find out. It does not mean that we must leave our own ways and adopt his. Now we must go on to the trader's. We left the sheep in the corral, for there was no one to tend them, and that is not as it should be."

As they went on, Sad Girl worried a little about the sheep. It was not like Grandmother to say that they should be left in the corral in the daytime. Each morning Sad Girl removed the long poles which served as a gate to the enclosure and waited for her small flock to amble forth. As she stood there she sang the special song which Navaho shepherds always sing when they release their charges from a night's captivity. Then she took them to graze, her hands ever busy with spinning, and watched over them until late afternoon. By the time she returned them to the corral, Grandmother had all the household chores attended to. She had brought in firewood and water, swept the dirt-floored hogan, aired the sheepskins which served as covers at night, and prepared the evening meal. There had been time, too, for her to add to the rug she was weaving in the loom beneath the brush shade.

This morning, however, Grandmother had broken the usual pattern of their existence. She had announced that the sheep would be left where they were. She was going to the trading post, and her granddaughter must go too. She did not give a reason for this expedition. The rug was not finished, nor was there wool to trade. There was still a little flour and a handful of coffee, so supplies, while low, need not be replenished. Grandmother had long since sold her turquoise and silver jewelry, so there was nothing to pawn or sell. Sad Girl was curious, but she did not ask questions.

She followed Grandmother's thin, straight back up the

single step of the trading post, lifting the dust ruffle of her long, full calico skirt so that it would not catch on the splintery wood.

The main room of the trading post was a delightful place. Two walls were lined with shelves stacked with canned goods, white man's blankets, and bolts of material—bright velvets and calico. From nails hung festoons of native jewelry, silver and turquoise and gleaming white shell, which the Indians were accustomed to pawn from time to time. Once in a while jewelry was sold outright, but usually the Navahos redeemed these treasures when they had money. On another wall were shelves holding articles which had been taken in trade, the beautiful hand-woven blankets made by the women, silver and turquoise jewelry designed for tourist trade, and boxes filled with fleece and spun yarn. In the back of the room was a long glass counter over which the trader and his customers bargained, and beneath the glass were the things which pleased Sad Girl most of all. Laid out in a mouth-watering array was a store of candy. There were paper-wrapped bars, but there were also containers filled with striped peppermint, pale orange marshmallow blobs, bright suckers, long black whips of licorice, and rainbow-hued gumdrops. It was seldom that they could afford to patronize this counter, but sometimes when Grandmother had finished her transaction the trader would slide back the glass and present a gumdrop or a peppermint to Sad Girl. And she could always look through the counter and imagine how things tasted without having to pay for the privilege.

Today Grandmother did not stop in the main room. She walked straight through and opened a door to the small office in back. Sad Girl followed closely at her heels, with only a wistful glance at the candy counter as she went by.

The trader was sitting at a table, making black marks on a piece of paper with a sharpened stick. He looked up and smiled at Grandmother and Sad Girl. No one said anything for some time, since it would not have been polite to begin immediately on the business which brought them there. At last, however, Grandmother spoke, and her mind was too full of the matter to speak of anything else.

"This one," she began, motioning to her granddaughter, "must go to the white man's school. She must go to the school which the children of Hosteen Yucca attend. She must learn to speak the white man's language. She must learn the best of the white man's ways. She must go at once before the nights begin to grow cold."

Sad Girl's eyes grew wide with astonishment and a little terror. She! Sad Girl! Go to the white man's school! Such an idea had never occurred to her, and she could find no place for it in her mind.

The trader scratched his head and looked thoughtfully from Sad Girl to the old grandmother.

"I know the government people came to talk to you

about this once," he said finally. "But can you spare her? You and your family have had much misfortune. More than most. Now you have only this little girl left. You need her with you to tend your sheep and bring in wood and water and to help in the hogan."

There was great pity in the trader's voice, for he had lived all his life near the Navahos. Sad Girl winced under his tone. Here it was again. Pity. She knew she should be humble and accept it, for that was what she had been born to, but something inside her refused to do so.

"My flock has dwindled. It is small," insisted Grandmother calmly. "I am not too old to herd six or eight sheep. And as I herd I can spin warp yarn to sell. I can bring in enough firewood and water for myself. With only one in the hogan it will not take so much water nor so large a fire. This one must go to the white man's school. The people who came to see me made marks on a paper. They know about my granddaughter. When I am gone she must know how to live side by side with the whites."

"There's no day school close," the trader reminded her. "She'd have to go to a boarding school, and the ones close to home are filled up early. If she goes to the one with the Yucca children it's a long way off. Many miles. I remember when Yucca first sent his girl away to school. She tried to get into one closer at home—Fort Sill, Tuba City. They're always filled first. Then they told her about Chemawa. It's a long way off, so it fills up last. She went there and liked it. Now her brother's going, too. They say it's a fine school, but it's a long journey and you wouldn't see your granddaughter again until summer. The time would be long."

"I won't go," said Sad Girl quickly.

Through her mind had flashed a picture of the weary, cold months when snow lay thickly on the ground. She imagined Grandmother struggling through the drifts to get wood and saw her sitting beside the small, smoking fire in the hogan, an occasional snowflake drifting down through the smoke hole in the top. There would be no one to talk with, no sound to break the stillness but the wind whipping against the dirt walls outside. She couldn't leave Grandmother. People felt pity that there were only two of them. What would they feel if she went away and left Grandmother all alone?

"That settles it then," said the trader, shrugging his shoulders. "They won't take children who don't want to go. There's enough of them who do want to. Over twenty-eight thousand of your Navaho children in government schools right now and wanting to be there. They've no time to bother with those who don't want to go."

Grandmother turned and looked at Sad Girl with a glance which seemed to pierce through her very skin.

"What kind of a granddaughter are you?" she asked scornfully. "Are you the kind who will not do as her mother's mother asks? Would you deny me this thing which makes me happy? This thing upon which I have set my heart? I have brought you up since you were born and have done the best I can for you in every way. I have shared with you everything that I have and taught you all that I know. Is this the way you reward me?"

Sad Girl was ashamed. Her eyes were not able to meet the stern black ones looking at her so accusingly.

"No, Grandmother," she said miserably. "I will do as you say. If you want me to go to the school, I will go."

Grandmother nodded her head in satisfaction. She turned once more to the trader. "Will you do what needs to be done? Will you tell the white people that this one is coming and ask that a place be made for her?"

"I'll do my best," he agreed hesitantly. "But don't set your heart on it. Not this year, anyway. She's not very old, is she?"

"She has seen twelve summers."

"They don't really want them till they're fourteen," he told her. "Start at fourteen, stay there five years, and when they're nineteen they've got a trade and are grown at the same time. That's the way they want it to work out."

"Perhaps she is fourteen," said Grandmother calmly. "One year is much like another to me. I may have mislaid a year or two. Tell them she is fourteen. The people who talked with me thought she was that age, and they may be right. But she must go in twice four days' time, which is when the cut-haired Yucca girl leaves."

Sad Girl knew then that she must go to the school. She must even pretend that she wanted to go. Some people

17

were rather careless about the truth. If they could benefit themselves by claiming that something was so when it was not, what did it matter? For three times in a row they would tell the same lie, and with so convincing an air that they were often believed. Grandmother was different. She never told an untruth. If she couldn't tell the truth, she closed her lips and said nothing at all. For her to tell a deliberate falsehood about Sad Girl's age could only mean that for some reason the white man's school was very important.

CHAPTER TWO

The Yuccas were mildly surprised when they heard that Sad Girl was to attend the boarding school, and if they secretly thought that she should stay on the reservation with her grandmother, they did not say so. They were generous, as always.

"If there were more time, the Tribal Council would have seen that she had clothing like the white people wear, but you decided too quickly for that," said Mrs. Yucca. "Grace has a dress which came from the school. She says she has outgrown it and that your granddaughter is welcome to have it. You will think it is lacking in fullness and also in length, but it is what the girls wear at the school."

"Your granddaughter must have a part in the Blessing Way which will be given for my daughter who returns to the school and for my son who goes there this year for the first time," insisted Hosteen Yucca. "It is not well to send our young people forth on a long journey without having the Blessing Way sung for them. I will tell the singer that the ceremonial is for your granddaughter as well as for my own children."

"You are very good," said Grandmother gratefully. She knew that the Blessing Way ceremonial was important, but she herself had no money to pay a singer.

Sad Girl accepted the offer of the dress and the ceremonial politely, but only because they made Grandmother happy. She couldn't feel real gratitude, not when she felt so sure the Yuccas' kindness was because they were sorry for her. If she and Grandmother only had a family of their own such things would have been taken care of. They might not have provided a new dress, for that was not so important. But someone, an aunt or uncle, even a distant cousin, would have paid a singer for the ceremonial. Families looked out for each other.

She did not tell anyone else of her feelings. She did not even speak of them to the sheep during that final week as she took the small flock out to graze. Perhaps it is the last time I will ever do this, she told herself. Who knows what will happen to me when I leave, what strange and terrifying dangers I will meet? The sheep, which had only been a responsibility before, now became very important to her. She looked at each one a long time and carefully, as though she wanted to make sure she would not forget a single thing about it. She looked at the brown plateau, studded with juniper, sage, and scanty grass, and at the encircling line of multicolored rock cliffs, designed like a Navaho blanket in masses of gray with stripings of red and black, orange and brown. This was her home, all that she had ever known, and while it had not brought

happiness, still it meant her life and a certain security. She was afraid to leave it.

The days raced by, and the one appointed for the Blessing Way arrived. Sad Girl had never had a Sing, and as she washed her long hair in yucca suds in preparation some of Grandmother's excitement carried over to her. But by the time she reached the Yuccas' hogan the excitement was gone. She sat dutifully beside Grace and watched as the sand painting was made on the floor. She listened to the sacred songs and thought about Changing Woman, the deity who had given this ceremony to the Navahos. There was a time when Changing Woman, like Sad Girl, was alone and without a family, but that had not been for long. Changing Woman had taken the Sun for a husband, and soon there were twin sons to bring her comfort. Therefore, the two cases were not alike at all. Even the Sun was proud to be the husband of Changing Woman, but Sad Girl herself never expected to be chosen by anyone. Men did not choose wives because they were sorry for them.

Hosteen Yucca had planned to drive his children, Grace and Tony, into Tuba City, which was the nearest center for enrollment in the boarding schools, and he said that Sad Girl might go with them. He invited Grandmother, too, but there was no one to take care of the sheep so she couldn't leave.

Sad Girl braided her long hair and put on the dress which Grace Yucca had given her, feeling very self-conscious as she did so. As Mrs. Yucca said, the skirt felt very skimpy indeed and much too short. Instead of the ten yards which went into the usual Navaho costume, this one could not have contained more than three or four. It was of cotton, in a shade of blue that Sad Girl did not greatly admire, and the skirt was not gathered but made with a pleat in front and another in the back. Worst of all, it did not come to the ground but ended at the center of her calf. There was a round white collar which came closely around her throat, with cuffs to match, and a cloth belt of the same material as the dress.

It was quite the ugliest dress Sad Girl had ever seen, and even Grandmother did not think it was pretty.

"Mrs. Yucca says that is what the girls wear," she remembered doubtfully. "You will not look strange to yourself when others are wearing the same thing."

The wagon stopped in front of the hogan, and Sad Girl climbed in with the Yucca children. The whole family was going into town to see them off. Mr. and Mrs. Yucca sat on the seat, while Grace, Tony, Mary, the oldest daughter, and her two small children occupied the wagon bed. Mary's husband had stayed at home to look after things while they were gone—a tactful arrangement, since if he had accompanied them Mrs. Yucca could not have gone. Custom demanded that a Navaho man and his mother-in-law avoid each other, and somehow they never came face to face after the marriage ceremony.

"Are you excited?" smiled Grace as Sad Girl climbed in and sat down on the rough boards beside her. "Are you scared? I was, the first time I went."

"Yes," said Sad Girl soberly.

"I'm not," declared Tony Yucca. "Not scared, I mean. But boys wouldn't be. I'm excited, though. I can hardly wait to get there, only I wouldn't want to miss the trip. That'll be fun, too."

"You won't think so," said Grace. "Not after the first day. You ride and ride and ride. They only stop to eat. You ride all day and all night and the next day and the next night. You get so tired of riding you can hardly stand it."

"Not me," denied Tony quickly. "I never get tired."

23

Sad Girl smiled weakly. She was not paying much attention to what they said. She was watching Grandmother, who stood in front of the hogan waiting for them to drive away. Her faded red calico skirt flapped around her ankles as the moving wheels stirred up a little breeze, and in the bright morning sunlight the ancient black velvet of her blouse showed up mottled in the spots where the pile of the material had worn away. But her graying head was high, her smile was brave encouragement, and her eyes were filled with pride. Sad Girl watched her as long as she could. The diminishing figure in the distance became only a red dot of color—the brightness of her skirt —then the dot, too, was gone.

She sighed without thinking and glanced over to catch Mary's eyes upon her.

"She will be here when you come back next summer," said Mary, nodding wisely. "When we had not been too long married my husband took me to visit his parents. They live many miles away, and we had to travel several days to get there. We were to stay all summer, and when it came time to leave I could hardly bear to go. I was afraid that while I was gone something would happen at home. That I would return and find that all was not as I left it."

"Yes," murmured Sad Girl. Under Mary's comforting smile she seemed to feel a little better. Mary had not been to school, but she seemed to understand better than Grace the things Sad Girl was thinking.

"You'll like it at Chemawa after you get used to it," Grace assured her. "At first it will be strange, but you'll get over that in a hurry."

"Tell us about it," urged Tony.

"I have told you. A hundred times."

"But not her," he argued, nodding toward Sad Girl. Then he was struck with a sudden idea. "She'll have to have a new name, so they can call her by it."

Sad Girl looked frightened. Navahos do not often tell their real names, for to use them too often would wear them out. The Yucca children, in fact most of the Navahos she knew, had white names also, but she and Grandmother had never considered such a thing.

"They'll give her one at the center," said Grace carelessly. "They always do, if anyone doesn't have one."

"Perhaps she would like to pick out her own," said Mary. "I did, years ago. There was a trader once, when I was a little girl, who had a good wife. She always smiled at us, and sometimes she gave us presents. I thought she was the kindest person in the world, and when I found out her name was Mary I asked if she would share the name with me. She said she was flattered that I wanted to use it, and she gave me permission."

"Do you know any name you'd like to have?" demanded Tony. "Any white name?"

Sad Girl shook her head. Mary was being very kind to her, and perhaps she should ask permission to share her name. But already it had been divided once. Possibly even

25

a white name should not be divided too often.

"Tell her some," Tony ordered Grace, and Grace good-naturedly began to list a few.

"Marjory, Eleanor, Sally, Martha, Alice——"

Sad Girl looked more frightened than ever, and Mary interrupted.

"Those names do not mean anything," she complained.

"Neither does your name," pointed out Tony. "Or mine, or Grace's. White names do not need to mean anything. They only make sounds."

"First names can mean something," said Grace superiorly. "Mine does. Grace means beauty or something like that. Sometimes they give names of jewels, Ruby, Pearl——"

"Turquoise?" asked Tony eagerly.

"I don't think so," frowned Grace. "Or flower names. I've heard flower names. But if she can't think of one, it doesn't matter. They'll pick one out for her. A first name and a last one. The last one will be for her grandmother to use, too. The same as our last name is Yucca."

Sad Girl felt more bewildered than ever. She wished she had known about this before, so she could have talked it over with Grandmother. It was too great a responsibility for her alone, having to select a family name. Even if the family was only two people it was an important decision. Some of her feelings must have shown on her face, for Mary added her urgings to Tony's.

"It will be better if she does it herself," she insisted.

26

"She should decide before she reaches the center. What if she doesn't like the name they give her?"

"All right," agreed Grace. "Do you want me to say some more names?"

"No," said Mary calmly. "Let us think. Flower names are used? This one is rather like a little flower."

Sad Girl grew warm with pleasure. She had never received a compliment before, and it made her feel glowing and shy at the same time.

"How about Daisy?" said Grace practically. "Or Violet? Or Rose?"

"Rose," repeated Mary quickly, looking at Sad Girl. "That is a nice name."

"Oh yes," agreed Sad Girl in a whisper. A white man's name might not be so bad as she imagined. Not if it could represent something so familiar and lovely as the fragrant pink blossom which perfumed the early summer. It was a good plant, too, for the wild rose had certain medicinal qualities.

"All right," agreed Grace. "That's your name. In English it's pronounced Rose. That is what you will be called at the school."

Sad Girl repeated the strange word several times, and Tony tried it too. It did not sound at all like the Navaho word for rose, but she realized that it meant the same thing.

"Now the second name," insisted Tony. "The name for her grandmother too."

"We are Yucca," said Mary. "Perhaps she could be Juniper or Cottonwood."

Grace shook her head.

"I have learned that the last name of most white men does not mean anything at all," she admitted. "Our last names do, when we have chosen them ourselves. It is not important that the last name mean anything. It does not describe."

Sad Girl felt a little relief at knowing this. Since the name must also apply to Grandmother, she had been very uneasy. Descriptions could sometimes be cruel. To the older Navahos and to the white trader Grandmother was known as She-Who-Knows-Much-Trouble.

"Then it doesn't matter," decided Tony promptly. "Let them pick it out at the center."

"No," said Sad Girl quickly. The people at the center might be accustomed to picking out names for children who had none, but it would be better to have one when she arrived. Perhaps they were sorry for those who had no names, and if she could do anything to avoid pity she meant to. "You choose for me, please. Choose now."

It was Grace's turn to look worried.

"I can't think of any except Smith," she admitted. "Smith is a white man's name."

"Is it all right for Rose to take it?" asked Mary anxiously.

"Of course."

"Then that's it," declared Tony with satisfaction.

"From now on you are to be called Rose Smith."

Rose Smith, who had once been Sad Girl, smiled shyly. She repeated the strange name, as Grace had taught her, several times. It had almost a gay lilt to it.

CHAPTER THREE

"Have you a white name by which you are called?" asked the interpreter at the center.

"Rose," she whispered a little fearfully. All the way into Tuba City she had been practicing it, learning to say it as Grace had taught her. She had become quite proficient, but it still sounded strange to her ears and she worried lest it might not be accepted.

The interpreter, however, did not question. He was a young Navaho, dressed like the wealthy whites in a dark business suit, white shirt, and striped necktie.

"And your second name?"

"Smith," she nodded, a little more confidently this time.

The interpreter turned and said "Rose Smith" to the white lady who was making black marks on a sheet of paper with one of those sharpened sticks like the trader used.

"Where are you from?" he asked. "Have you applied for admittance before? Have we a record on you?"

"She lives near us," explained Grace Yucca, who by virtue of her own past experience had volunteered to help

Tony and Rose register. "I am Grace Yucca. I go to Chemawa for the third year. My brother Tony goes for the first time. Rose also goes for the first time. She is fourteen. The trader, Mr. Johnson, who has the post at Goose Hollow, said he would write about Rose to tell you that she was coming. People from the government came to see her grandmother this summer about getting her into the school."

"Oh," said the interpreter, frowning a little. He turned and spoke rapidly to the lady at the table. She put down her sharpened stick and began running through papers on the table. After a while she found the one she must have been looking for, and she, too, frowned and spoke to the interpreter in English.

Rose shivered as she watched their faces and listened to the strange, unintelligible words which she could not understand. Grace must have known what they were saying, however, and Grace did not look worried. She stood, as she had before, smiling politely, waiting for them to finish. At last the interpreter spoke to Rose in Navaho.

"The paper which the white trader wrote about you is here. It does not give your name, but it says that a new girl from the district around Goose Hollow post is coming. He should have waited until he had an answer from us before he told you to start out. There are so many children who want to go to the schools, we cannot find places for them all."

Grace Yucca began to speak to the interpreter and the

white woman in English. Rose couldn't understand the words but she knew what Grace was saying, for the white woman shook her head pityingly and her tongue went "tsk, tsk, tsk." Grace was saying that Rose had to go to the school. That she was an orphan, with no family to take care of her, and that she had no place else to go. Rose wanted to cry out that it wasn't true. She did have some place to go. She could go home, to the round little hogan, to the sheep on the juniper-dotted plain, to Grandmother. Her mouth grew dry with shame, and she said nothing.

When Grace was finished, the interpreter and the white woman conferred. The woman looked at her papers again and made marks with the blackening stick. Then she said something in a loud voice and the interpreter shrugged his shoulders.

"You may go to the school," he told Rose. "A place will be made for you. Go into the next room now and see the doctor."

Rose opened the door to which he pointed, and stepped into the doctor's office. This time Grace Yucca did not go with her and she felt very much alone. There was no special interpreter in this room, for the nurse was a young Navaho woman who smiled at her encouragingly.

The doctor was bald, and Rose stared at his shining pink scalp in amazement. Goose Hollow was one of the more isolated districts, with such poor roads that few white people went there. She had never before seen anyone with no hair at all. He wore a starched jacket of unbelievable whiteness, but the strangest thing about him was that he looked out through two small round panes of glass, one over each eye. They were held in place with gold wire which ran back to hook over his ears.

"Hello," said the nurse briskly. "How are you called?"

"Rose Smith."

"How old are you, Rose?"

"Fourteen."

"You're small for fourteen," said the nurse critically. "Come and sit in this chair. The doctor will examine you to see that you are in good health."

Rose sat in the chair. The doctor placed a little metal disk on her chest, to which were attached black thongs. He put the other end of the thongs to his ear and nodded his head approvingly. He looked into her eyes and down her throat.

"Now I'm going to take a little blood from your arm," said the nurse. "By examining the blood we can make sure there are no hidden sicknesses which may someday appear. It will hurt for just a moment when I put in the needle, then it will be all over."

Rose tried to keep her arm from trembling as the nurse washed off a little place on the skin with bottled water which felt colder than any she had ever known.

"How old did you say you were?" asked the nurse. A long, sharp needle was coming close to the cold place on her arm.

33

"Fourteen," said Rose, and the needle bit into her skin. On the other end of the needle was a slim little jar which began filling with dark red fluid.

"I didn't hear," said the nurse calmly. "How old did you say?"

"Fourteen," repeated Rose, and then with a rising horror which made her forget the sharp needle she realized that she had now told the lie three times.

Three times was all right. Three times was safe. But the Navaho who tells the same lie four times is subject to great danger, for now the circle is complete. The four lies could come at her from every side—north, south, east, and west —to overwhelm her.

"That's all," said the nurse. She stuck the wet bit of cotton on the prick in Rose's arm. "Clench your fist and double up your arm. It will stop bleeding in a moment."

Rose did as she was told. Again the wet cotton felt cold but it did not hurt.

"Now," said the Navaho nurse. "How old are you, Rose?"

"Twelve," she whispered miserably.

"I thought so." The nurse turned and spoke rapidly to the doctor in English. To Rose's surprise, the doctor was not angry. He only grinned and said something which the nurse interpreted. "You should have told me the truth in the beginning. I knew you were only twelve. The doctor knew it. Anyone would, by looking at you, for you are small even for that."

34

"Shall I go home?" She felt a certain relief. Grandmother would understand that she could not tell the lie four times.

"Oh no." The nurse shook her head and began putting things away. "The schools ask that the children be fourteen when they come, but they won't send you back once you are there. You won't be the only twelve-year-old, either. There are half a dozen others who have managed to get through registrations."

The rest of the day was a series of strange and unexpected experiences. People kept asking her questions and making tests. She was provided with more clothing, panties, a shirt, and a cotton slip, all to go under the blue dress which Grace had given her. To Rose this was a great extravagance, for all these garments were worn out of sight, and the sun was hot enough so she did not need them for warmth. She was given a sweater, too, but what impressed her most of all was a pair of shoes. She had always worn moccasins, and the leather oxfords which laced up over her instep felt heavy and unyielding. She was conscious of them with every step, and she had a little trouble getting used to them. But they made her feel very elegant, and she only wished Grandmother could see them.

"I will tell her about them," smiled Mary. "I will tell your grandmother that you now have fine leather shoes like the whites wear and a pair of stockings to wear under them."

The Yuccas were camped overnight at the edge of town, and the children had gone back to spend the night with them. Accommodations at the center were crowded, and any parent who wished to take care of his own children was permitted to do so. The big busses would leave early the next morning, and Tony was already afraid they would oversleep and be too late.

"Early to the white man is late to us," Grace assured him. "You will learn. At school, when the rising bell sounds, the girls in our wing have been up a long time. We have cleaned our rooms and done our work by the time the white people are ready to get up."

She proved to be right, and when they arrived at the

center the next morning the busses had not yet arrived. The streets were crowded with Navahos. It was easy to tell the older boys and girls who were returning to Chemawa for the second, third, or fifth year, for they were laughing and chattering as they greeted each other after a summer's parting. All of them had been working, some in town, others on farms or ranches, and a few had been helping out with the flocks of sheep owned by their own families. Each had a great deal of assurance, Rose decided, and seemed happy to be returning. Perhaps the white school was not such a frightening place as she imagined. The younger children, starting out for the first time, were more subdued. Even Tony, who had scarcely been able to wait, was a little fearful, now that the time of departure was at hand.

The busses arrived before long. They were huge affairs painted gray, with a picture of a running dog on the side, and they seemed to make a terrifying amount of noise. The Indians fell back as they pulled up at the curb, and the noise stopped. Three interpreters pushed their way through the crowd, and each took up a stand before the door of one of the busses.

"Older students take busses one and two," came a loud voice over the murmur of the crowd. "New students take bus three."

"Thank you," whispered Rose, looking at Hosteen Yucca and his wife. "Thank you for everything. Please tell my grandmother——" At this moment she could think of no message for Grandmother.

"We will tell her that you are on your way," promised Mary quickly. "We will tell her that you are well and that you have new shoes like those carried in the trading post. We will tell her that you are going to be a credit to her."

Rose looked into Mary's gentle brown eyes and somehow found the courage to make herself turn and find a place in the line of new students waiting to board the bus. At the door the interpreter asked her name and made a mark on a paper before he motioned for her to enter.

She had never before seen anything like the interior of the bus. There was a place for the driver in front, and an extra wheel ran up from a pole in front of him. She did not know the reason for this wheel. It was smaller than those on the outside of the bus, but perhaps it was a spare. If something went wrong with one of the regular wheels, perhaps this could be used in some way.

There were two rows of seats, with an aisle between, running the length of the bus, and the children were settling themselves, everyone trying to get next to a window. Those behind her kept pushing her on, and she was almost in the back before she realized that she must find a seat for herself. Tony was nowhere to be seen, and he wouldn't want to sit with a girl anyway. Luckily she saw a girl sitting alone next to a window, and hurried to take the seat beside her. The girl did not look up. She had her nose pressed against the glass, staring out at the crowd, and every once in a while she raised her hand and waved to someone.

This was only the second time in her life that Rose had occupied one of the white man's chairs, raised on legs off the floor. She had sat on the one in the doctor's office during registration, but that seat had been made of smooth wood. It was hard and unyielding. This was soft and padded as though it were filled with freshly sheared fleece. The trader always sat on a seat raised from the floor by four sticks, and from her own cross-legged place on the floor she had imagined it would feel awkward. It didn't at all.

She sat quietly, marveling at this new experience, and waited for the bus to fill. She saw that those who had extra belongings were stowing things away on a shelf near the top of the bus. She had nothing except what she had on her back, and for a moment she was sorry she had not brought a souvenir to remind her of home. There had been nothing to bring, however, and, besides, she needed no reminder of home. She would not forget.

Finally the last passenger was aboard. Every seat was filled. The driver swung the door shut and did something which started the noisy voice of the bus. Slowly they began to move. Those next to the windows waved harder than ever, and everyone but Rose leaned forward to catch a final glimpse of the families they were leaving. She sat quietly waiting, not knowing exactly what to expect.

At first they went very slowly, then they began to go faster. Buildings raced by so quickly that she had no time to examine them. This was a disappointment, for she had never been to town before. The buildings grew fewer and fewer, and they went faster than ever. It was like flying, only they stayed on the ground. It made her feel happy and excited to ride so fast, and she wasn't frightened at all.

The girl in the seat beside her turned finally and looked at Rose. For the first few blocks after they had left the center she had kept her nose determinedly pressed against the glass. Then she had looked straight ahead without turning her head, but her eyelashes had blinked very rapidly. Rose thought she must be trying to keep back tears. Now, however, she smiled in a friendly fashion.

"Hello."

Rose shook her head apologetically and answered in Navaho.

"I do not speak the white man's language."

"Neither do I," confided the girl instantly. "Only a few words. The trader at the post nearest us taught us that before we left. He said if we said hello and smiled people would be friendly."

"I will remember," agreed Rose thoughtfully. "It will be a help to know some words."

"I think so too. There will be so much to learn when we arrive that anything we can learn before will be a help. Do you know any of their words at all?"

"Only my name."

"What is your name?"

"Rose. Rose Smith."

"Rose Smith!" cried the girl in delight. "That is part of my name. My name is Lucy Smith. Perhaps we are of the same family."

CHAPTER FOUR

The soft padded seats of the bus, which Rose thought so
luxurious, grew very hard and uncomfortable before they
arrived at their destination. They traveled two days and
two nights, with only five short stops a day. Everyone
rushed to get out at each halt, and there was much stamp-
ing of feet and stretching of aching muscles.

Rose considered that she was very fortunate in her seat
partner, for Lucy Smith was a friendly girl and far more
experienced than Rose herself. Lucy had ridden in auto-
mobiles before. She explained the use of the extra wheel
in front of the driver. She knew the names of some of the
strange foods which they were served three times a day
at restaurants along the highway. She even knew something about the school to which they were going, things
which Grace Yucca had not bothered to explain.

It was in a place called Oregon, a great many miles
away from Arizona, which was the state in which they
lived. Rose had not even known that her home country had
a special name, much less that it was Arizona. Nor would
they be so completely cut off from their families as Rose
had imagined, for there were such things as letters to be

sent. Letters were pieces of paper with writing on them which would tell of the things which were happening to them at school. One of the things they would learn first was to make this kind of writing.

"But what good will it do?" Rose wondered. "Who will care to read it after I have learned to write?"

"Your family," smiled Lucy wisely. "They will want to know what you are doing."

"They do not know how to read it."

"The trader will. Your family will take the letter, when it comes, to the trader, and he will tell them what it says. Then they will tell him what has been happening to them, and he will write it on a paper and send it to you. Then you will know how things are with your family."

"That is fine," agreed Rose soberly. She had not confessed to Lucy that her only family consisted of one person.

She had felt warm and happy when Lucy had exclaimed that with the same last name they must be related. Of course, they had both known it wasn't so. Lucy's name had been assigned to her, a haphazard selection at best. They couldn't belong to the same family. But what a comforting feeling it was when Lucy called her "Younger Sister" as she had taken to doing.

Rose was learning other things from her new friend as well. Lucy laughed a great deal. She made little jokes about the discomforts, such as a foot which went to sleep or the stuffiness of the bus. Rose had never had anyone

43

to laugh with before. The Navahos are a cheerful, good-natured people, but she had always withdrawn herself from the others. She had never realized how good it was to share an idea with someone else.

The new school held no terrors for Lucy, in spite of the fact that she was the first of her family to go so far away. Her home was in a district more populated than the area around Goose Hollow. Her older brothers and sisters had attended a day school, and her mother had gone there to use the laundry facilities. The ways of the people with white skins did not seem so frightening to her, and a little of Lucy's attitude rubbed off on Rose.

They traveled across deserts and through forests, traversed towns and cities and lush countryside. Sometimes the highway skirted deep, swift-moving rivers, and these were the most amazing sights of all to the children who had never seen so much water in a stream at one time. From the windows they sometimes caught glimpses of white-capped peaks glistening under a blue sky, and that was astonishing too. Whoever had heard of snow so deep and cold that the summer's sun could not melt it all? There was a great deal to see and to marvel about, but they all breathed a sigh of relief when the driver finally turned and made a loud announcement. They could not understand the words, but there was no mistaking his meaning, and the children cheered.

They were on the last lap of the journey. Before very long they would be in Chemawa.

The bus turned off the main highway onto a narrow country road. On either side was farm land, tilled fields and pastures, the like of which these former shepherds had never seen. What their hungry sheep wouldn't have given for this long, thick grass!

Ahead lay a cluster of buildings. In the late afternoon sun they glowed warmly red, like the design in a blanket. The children pressed their noses against the windows to see better as the bus came to a stop.

There were a great many of the brick buildings, set back from the street, with narrow paths running up to them. A railroad track ran straight through the center of the community, and, as they learned later on, when this was in use all classwork and conversation had to wait until the noisy freight rolled by. Behind the school buildings was a row of small frame houses, most of them painted a tidy white, which housed the faculty. Tall trees, mainly firs and maple, cast cooling shade over green lawns, and between two of the taller buildings Rose had a glimpse of boys playing some kind of a game with rackets and balls.

She filed out of the bus with the others and then shyly held back, waiting for Lucy to join her. The sidewalk became filled with children, but there were not so many as she had imagined there would be. At appointed stations along the highway their own busses had been joined by those from different centers on the reservation, until they now made a caravan of eleven busses in all. She did not

45

know that some of them were deliberately held back to arrive at twenty-minute intervals and make assignment to dormitories more simple.

"What do we do now?" whispered Rose, her old terror returning.

"Just wait. Someone will tell us," said Lucy confidently.

And someone did. Little by little, group by group, they were sorted out. Rose gave a gasp of relief when she discovered that she and Lucy were not to be separated. She was afraid that the two years' difference in their ages would do this automatically.

"All first-year girls follow me," called a young Navaho woman clearly. "You will live in McBride Hall."

Clinging together, Lucy and Rose fell into the line of younger girls forming on the walk. Almost a fourth of the new arrivals were there for the first time. The interpreter started down one of the paths, and the girls followed. Many of them carried belongings in suitcases, paper bags, and flour sacks, but Rose noticed with relief that she was not the only one to arrive empty-handed.

At one of the red brick buildings they mounted a short flight of stairs, crossed a wooden porch, and came into a large room which made her blink with amazement. She didn't know that it was old and bravely made over. She saw only the bright paint and fresh curtains, and she found it hard to believe she was going to live in all this luxury. The walls were paneled in wood which had been painted white. There was a rug on the floor, so large that she marveled at the size of the loom which must have made it. Instead of stripes and a conventional design, the rug had roses woven into it, a feat for any weaver. There were many chairs, some large enough to hold more than one person, with bright cushions on them, and tables, with flowers in vases. There was a place for the fire, too, but it was not in the center of the room but against one wall, and the smoke hole was enclosed and ran up to the roof out of sight.

"This is Mrs. Masters, your matron, girls," said the interpreter.

They all turned and stared at a smiling, middle-aged white woman. She had always eaten well and showed it.

She was good-tempered and wished to be their friend. She showed that, too, and they all returned her smile. She said something to the interpreter.

"Mrs. Masters says she knows you are hungry," translated the interpreter. "She says you have had a long trip and must be tired. There is still much to be done before you are settled in your new home, but she thinks you will feel more like it after you have eaten."

The new students smiled and nodded at Mrs. Masters, who smiled and nodded back.

"Follow me to the bathroom," continued the interpreter. "There you can wash your hands and faces. Then I will show you the cafeteria. Supper is ready and waiting for you."

The bathroom was another wonder. Very few of the new students understood about turning faucets on and off, and the interpreter first gave a demonstration. After that they took their turns at the basins, taking great delight in turning the two mysterious handles, one of which disgorged hot water, the other cold. All the while they chattered in excitement.

So much water! Is there no end to it? Where does it come from? Be saving, now. Everything must have an end. It would be a pity to drain the water dry just because there seems to be so much!

They were enthusiastic about the soap. Their own soap was made by pounding the yucca plant, and a few of them had never even seen cake soap before. It was slippery to the touch, and that caused no small merriment, but the lather it produced brought forth much excitement. Besides, it had a nice smell, a smell which lingered on the hands even after they were rinsed and dried. They filed out of the bathroom, sniffing in astonished pleasure and commenting on the fact.

Odors of good food greeted them as they reached the cafeteria door, and Rose felt her mouth begin to water. In all the excitement of arrival she had forgotten how hungry she was. The line of girls, which had moved along at a brisk rate, now began to slow down as they waited to be served.

"I hope they don't run out of food before they come to us," said Lucy anxiously.

Rose hoped so too. Boys were filing in the opposite door, and the two lines seemed alarmingly long. With so many to feed, the possibility of a shortage did not seem too remote.

At last they reached the long serving table. Someone put a metal tray in Rose's hand. Someone else gave her a handful of silverware. She accepted this dutifully, but outside of the spoon she did not consider the silver necessary. The sort of knife used by white people at table was too dull to cut tough meat. Forks were superfluous.

A lady in a white apron leaned across the counter and presented each girl with a filled plate. There was stew on it, made of meat, vegetables, and thick gravy, a slice of bread spread with something yellow, a canned peach on a green leaf with a ball of white lumpy substance beside it. Rose was glad to see the stew as well as the canned peach, which she esteemed as a great luxury. She was not so sure about the other food.

As they moved on, someone placed on their trays small dishes filled with something that was brown and of a creamy texture.

"Chocolate!" recognized Lucy in delight. "Like candy."

Last of all, they accepted, a little reluctantly, a glass of milk. They had learned after two days on the bus when meals were ordered for them that they were expected to drink milk. Few of them cared for it, but they drank it out of politeness. Had they been allowed to choose a beverage, it would have been coffee, which they had been drinking since they were young.

Lucy and Rose found places together at one of the tables, carried their trays over, and sat down.

"Let's eat the chocolate first," suggested Lucy, her eyes shining in anticipation.

They ate the pudding first, then the peach, the stew, and the bread. The white lumpy food served with the peach they found rather lacking in flavor, but they ate that, too, lest they be thought discourteous, and finally drank the milk.

After supper one of the interpreters took small groups on tours of the building, while the others stayed in the bright sitting room with the matron, attending to that mysterious business called "getting settled." Lucy and

Rose were among the first groups to go on tour, and even the experienced Lucy was impressed.

There was something named a Recreation Room, where they could relax after school, with paint even brighter than the downstairs sitting room. There was a big table, with a low net strung across the middle, which was used in playing some kind of game. There was a wooden box with handles, and when one of these handles was turned, music filled the air, although no one was playing the instrument. There were magazines with many pictures to look at, cushioned chairs to sit in, gay strips of cloth hanging at the glass windows.

The laundry room was equally amazing. Here were tubs which could be filled with water from faucets, but there were also machines which ran by themselves to do the scrubbing. It did not have to be done by hand. Moreover, there were rollers to squeeze the moisture from wet garments. All one had to do was turn a crank. The interpreter assured them that there was plenty of water. It was without end, and they were expected to use it freely. The Navahos smiled joyfully at that. Imagine all the water anyone could wish for, without having to carry it a long way in a bucket.

When they took a bath, and they were expected to do so often—that very night, in fact, before they went to bed —they simply stood under a little silver disk, turned a handle, and water poured down over their whole bodies. Most of them wanted to try it then and there, but they were told it must wait. They walked down a long corridor, where doors stood open at either side.

"One of these rooms will be yours," said the interpreter. She stood back to let them crowd the doorway to peer in. "The younger girls are usually assigned four or six to a room. But when you have been here longer and are one of the older girls, you will have only one roommate."

The rooms were not lavishly furnished nor as colorful as the sitting rooms, but they seemed very rich and imposing. There was a chest of drawers, topped by a mirror in which one could see one's whole face and upper part of one's body at once. There were some ordinary chairs, and the beds were built in tiers, one over another. They were covered with gay cotton material to match the curtains, and Rose, who was used to sleeping under a sheepskin, hoped they would be warm enough when the weather turned chill.

At last they returned to the sitting room, for it was their turn to be "settled." A new interpreter stood with the matron, translating the Navaho answers of the children into English. This was the youngest, prettiest interpreter Rose had yet seen. She could not have been much more than twenty. Her black hair had been coaxed to curl around her face, and her brown eyes twinkled with almost as much excitement as those of the children. She wore a white blouse, and a full flowered skirt was belted around a tiny waist.

"I'm Miss Fox," she told Rose, when it was her turn to

come to the table. "And how are you to be called?"

"Rose Smith."

Mrs. Masters, who had been listening carefully, beamed and nodded at the name. Her finger ran down a line of writing on the paper before her.

"Of course, Rose," said Miss Fox. "I've been looking for you. You're to be in my group. My class."

Rose did not understand what Miss Fox meant, but she was happy that she was to be with this pretty interpreter in any capacity.

"You're twelve, aren't you?" continued Miss Fox. "We're going to have twenty-three twelve-year-olds here this year. They'll all be together for studies in one class-room, and I'll be the teacher-interpreter in that room. I'll stay with your class for three years, and by then you won't need me any more. You'll understand everything that's said and will be speaking better than I do now."

Rose smiled politely. Miss Fox was going to be fun. She liked to make jokes. Then the interpreter said something which made her wonder if she hadn't been mistaken after all.

"Ten of my students are girls, and you'll all live in this dormitory. You're going to share a room with three of your classmates."

The smile faded from Rose's face. What she had been afraid of was happening. She was to be separated from her one friend, Lucy Smith. She was going to live with three strangers.

53

CHAPTER FIVE

Rose had never felt so lost and miserable as when she followed Miss Fox down the hall. It was even worse than when she left home, because then she had never had a special friend her own age. Now she had one, Lucy Smith, and Lucy was about to be torn from her. She didn't want to room with strangers. They might be unfriendly. They might even be the sort to pry, and when they found out she had no family they would feel sorry for her.

Lucy never pried. She gave her friendship freely and asked no questions. Lucy hadn't wanted to be separated either and had tried to talk her way out of it.

"Rose is my sister. My younger sister. We should be together."

"You will see her often. Every day," consoled Miss Fox. "But you are fourteen and will be in a beginning class with those of the same age. Your sister will be happier with the twelve-year-olds, once she gets to know them."

But she never would, Rose told herself helplessly. There would never be another friend like Lucy Smith.

They had given Rose a neat pile of new belongings to take to her room. There were white towels, several of them, and washcloths for her individual use. There was a tiny brush on a little stick, with which she was supposed to scour her teeth night and morning, and something called a comb, with which she was supposed to smooth out her hair. There were extra clothes too. They told her that the dress she was wearing was very pretty but that one was not quite enough. She needed two and another set of underwear as well. This was because she must always wear clean clothing, and when one outfit was being laundered she would have another to put on. They provided her with a coat, because soon the days would be colder, and a sweater would not keep her warm.

"You will want more things before long," said Miss Fox, "but these must do for now. We do not have a great stock, and we like our boys and girls to earn their own clothes. There are many jobs around the school, and you will be paid for the extra work you do. You can buy the things you need by working."

Rose smiled politely. Why should anyone need more than this? She could have done with far less. Especially could she have done without the two-piece garment with legs which they insisted upon giving her. It was called pajamas and was to wear while she slept under the covers. This was one of those foolish customs of the whites which she would never bother to carry home.

Her roommates were already in the room when they arrived, and Miss Fox introduced them.

"This is Dolores and Maria. Over here is Isobel. Girls,

this is your fourth roommate, Rose. She is from Arizona.
Dolores and Maria are both from New Mexico, and Isobel
comes from Utah, so you're all true Southwesterners."

Dolores and Maria smiled, but Isobel only stared. I'm
not going to like that one, decided Rose quickly. She
thinks she's better than anybody else.

Isobel was larger than the other twelve-year-olds in the
room, and she must have come from a well-to-do family.
Besides a wide turquoise bracelet, she wore matching earrings and a necklace. Her face was rather plain, and Rose
thought she looked proud and a little disdainful. She
was sitting quietly on one of the bunks, her brown hands

folded in her lap.

Dolores and Maria were quite different from Isobel and looked enough alike to be sisters. Rose glanced at them again and decided they must be sisters, twins undoubtedly, since they were both twelve. They were short and round, with dimples in their cheeks, and they giggled at everything which was said. They seemed to be friendly, and for a moment she felt comforted. Perhaps they would be like Lucy. Then, as Miss Fox turned to go, closing the door behind her, they turned eagerly to each other and began talking as they had before. Her heart sank. The twins had no need for an outsider.

Rose stood quietly, holding her stack of belongings. She didn't know what to do next. Isobel was regarding her appraisingly. The twins were giggling over some private joke. She wet her lips, which had become dry and parched.

"What—what do they want me to do with these?" she asked finally.

Isobel said nothing, and the twins broke off to stare for a moment. Then they were convulsed with new laughter.

"We'll show you," said Dolores, running to the chest of drawers. "See, there are hidden boxes in here. They are called draw-ers. They pull out like this. You put your things in them. One of them is for you alone."

"I have the top one," explained Maria, "and Dolores has the one just below. Isobel took the bottom one, so this is yours. After you have put your things inside you close it up, and no one can see."

"It looks neat that way," observed Rose shyly. The twins seemed pleased to explain about the drawers. Perhaps they weren't so bad after all.

"And that is your bed," continued Dolores, pointing. "It is the top one above where Isobel is sitting. I sleep in the other top one, and Maria sleeps beneath me. I chose it because I think it will be fun to sleep up high. But Isobel was here before you and had first choice of those beds. She took the one underneath. Perhaps she was afraid she would fall out in the night."

"Oh, Dolores!" giggled Maria. "You're so funny!"

At that the twins seemed to forget about her. Rose made neat piles of the towels and underwear and closed the drawer.

"You aren't supposed to put your dress and coat in there," said Isobel suddenly. Her voice was hoarse, and it seemed critical to Rose's sensitive ears. "There's a little room for them. Open that door and you'll see."

Rose flushed, and the twins laughed uproariously at the joke.

"We forgot to tell you," admitted Maria. "And so did the interpreter. She told us, or we wouldn't have known about it, either."

"This room is a clos-et," said Dolores, opening a door. Her hand reached up to a bar for a wire hanger. "This is called a hang-er. If people keep on telling us names of things we'll know all the white man's words we need before we even get to class."

"Caf-e-ter-ia," pronounced Maria carefully. "That's a funny one."

It was true, Rose realized with surprise. Ever since she arrived she had been learning names of things. Grandmother would be very proud of her. She wondered what Grandmother was doing at this moment. It was growing dark outside, so she must be in the hogan, sitting all alone. A lump came in her throat, and she deliberately made herself think of something else.

She slipped her new dress and coat on hangers, as Dolores showed her how to do, and hung them on the bar

59

with the other garments. She noticed that Isobel's clothes took up the most room in the closet. Isobel must have arrived with a large suitcase from home. The twins were busy at the chest of drawers, taking out articles and enjoying themselves thoroughly.

"We're going to bed," explained Maria. "At least we're going to put on these pajamas they gave us and use the little brushes for our teeth."

"We get to wash again, too," remembered Dolores. "We get to stand under the water and let it run all over us."

"And use the soap that smells sweet," cried Maria.

"Do you care if I come with you?" asked Rose shyly.

"Of course not," said Dolores in a surprised tone. "Come with us if you want to."

The twins were polite and friendly enough, but she still felt like an outsider all the while she walked down the corridor beside them. She couldn't enter into their private jokes, and they talked mostly to each other.

Once they reached the shower room, however, she didn't care. Lucy was there with her new roommates. Lucy was lucky. Her roommates were all friendly, and if they treated Rose a little condescendingly because she was two years younger it didn't matter. She stood in line with them waiting her turn at the shower. Then she dashed under the warm spray, and as she felt it run down her back and over her shoulders she knew true luxury. So much water! Warm and cleansing, it streamed down her body and ran wastefully away in little holes in the floor. Nobody cared about the waste, either. She lathered herself with the soap and let the warm water wash it away.

"Hurry up," called the girls waiting in line. "You've had your turn."

She had to come out, and now she saw that the white towels were to dry off the extra water. They felt soft to her skin, unlike the harsh sand which was used to dry the steaming body after a sweat bath at home.

She could hardly wait now to try on the scorned pajamas. Other girls were wearing them, and they were causing much amusement. To wear pants like a man and above all to wear such things when everyone was sleeping!

"But perhaps their blankets are not so warm as sheepskins and we would be cold without," considered Lucy practically. "It will not always be summer weather, and I have only seen one place for a fire in the whole building."

The twins had gone back to the room without her, and Rose reluctantly tore herself away from Lucy. The lights had flickered as they were using the tiny brushes on their teeth, and someone had explained it was meant as a signal. Soon lights would go out all over the building, and by then everyone must be in bed.

The twins were already in their bunks as she opened the door, but Isobel was still sitting on the side of hers. She had wrapped herself in a beautiful Navaho blanket, undoubtedly brought with her from home, and her fingers were stroking a fold of the firmly woven wool.

"Hurry, hurry," called Maria. "Get into bed. Soon it will be dark."

"It is very nice up here," Dolores assured her, beaming down from the top bunk. "There are two blankets on every bed, and two big squares of white cloth underneath, and a pillow for your head. One of the girls in the shower told us you are supposed to sleep between the white cloths. They are called sheets."

Rose hurried to climb into her bunk. She had to step on Isobel's bed and swing herself up to do so. The bed was soft and padded, as the seats in the bus had been. She rather doubted that she would be able to sleep on such softness. It would probably grow uncomfortable before morning, as the bus seats had done after she sat on them a long time. She folded down the blankets and for the first time in her life slid in between white sheets.

"Aren't you going to bed, Isobel?" called Dolores.

"You can't sit there all night," giggled Maria. "It will be dark in a minute."

"I'm not afraid of the dark," said Isobel. "I like it."

The lights went out as she spoke, and the twins twittered with delight and excitement.

After a few moments Rose heard Isobel moving around in the darkness below her. There was no sound of a drawer being opened, so Isobel must not be trying out her new pajamas. The lower bunk creaked with her weight as she climbed in, then everything was quiet save for an occasional muffled titter from one of the twins.

Rose lay straight in her new soft bed, wondering when it would begin to grow uncomfortable. She fell asleep still thinking about it.

CHAPTER SIX

Classes did not start the next day. There was no time for them. Right after breakfast Miss Fox gathered up her group of twelve-year-olds and told them they would stay together during the day. She would explain things as they went along. Rose looked curiously at the faces of these boys and girls with whom she would spend so much time. It was frightening to be with so many strangers, and she wondered if she would ever get used to it.

First there was a meeting of all the new students. A white lady, who was in charge of the Navaho program, spoke to them through an interpreter. She told them she was happy they had come to Chemawa on the special Five-Year Program for Navahos.

Rose had never heard of the Five-Year Program, but fortunately the lady explained what it was. On the reservation there are many hundreds of boys and girls from twelve to eighteen who have never been to school. They do not know English. They do not know how to take care of their health. They do not know how to find jobs. Many of them will want to go away to work in a few years, because the reservation is not large enough to support them all. They will want to earn their livings, and to do all this they must go to school.

These boys and girls cannot start in a regular school and finish high school. The regular school takes twelve years to finish. It starts with young children who are six years old. A fourteen-year-old can get only five years of schooling before he is old enough to work, and he does not want to go to classes with children who are younger. They do not like to do the same things.

Small children must go slowly in their education because they are young. Older boys and girls must learn some things very fast, and they must do everything in five years.

In the first three years they must learn to speak some English, to read and write and work arithmetic. They must learn good manners and good health. They must learn about things which are going on in the world, some of the laws of the country, and how to use them. They must learn how to use the school bank, about taxes and how to pay just the right amount. Boys go to shop classes every day for an hour and a half and learn how to use and care for tools. Girls spend the same amount of time in home economics classes, where they learn to make their own clothes, prepare good meals, and care for small children.

Rose, who had been sitting with the other twelve-year-olds who would be in her class, shook her head hopelessly. There was so much to learn. She didn't know whether she would be able to master it all. She glanced over and caught Miss Fox's eyes upon her. Miss Fox smiled and nodded encouragingly, as though she knew what Rose was thinking. Miss Fox must believe it could be done, so Rose smiled back, determined to do the best she could.

"When the student is finishing his third year, he must choose a special kind of work by which he will earn his living," continued the white lady. "Some of you boys will want to be farmers, or dairymen, mechanics, or perhaps bakers. There are many other kinds of work that boys may learn. Girls may choose to work in the home or to work in hospitals or factories. There are just as many things for girls to do.

"Each of you will be trained how to do the work which you have chosen. It is up to you to work hard to excel in your profession. When you have completed your classwork and have learned all you can from us, the school will find you a job. The people who hire you will pay money for your services; then you can live as you choose."

Rose listened carefully as the interpreter told them what the white lady was saying. The last part was even harder for her to understand than the first part. She had never thought of doing anything different from the things she had always done. She could imagine no other life besides that of living with Grandmother in the hogan, tending the sheep, spinning and weaving on one of the rugs which replaced each other in endless succession on the loom. She hoped they wouldn't ask her to choose a profession right

66

away. She wouldn't know how to go about choosing one.

After the meeting there was a tour of other buildings, a glimpse into their new classroom, and several demonstrations. One of these was on how to use the equipment in the laundry and was given by one of the elder students in the school. When one of the new pupils timidly inquired if she were a regular teacher like Miss Fox, the girl grinned and shook her head.

"No. I need a new pair of shoes. That's why I'm doing this. Six hours of work for the school, and I'll get a new pair of brown-and-white saddles."

"But you have shoes," pointed out one of the children in amazement.

Every eye in the group was on the demonstrator's feet. True, her serviceable oxfords had seen much service, but there were no rips in the leather.

"Oh, these old things," she said disdainfully. "They're all right for school, but I can hardly wear them when I dress up or go to town, can I? And it's the only pair of shoes I have. What if I got my feet wet?"

The first-year girls looked at each other in bewilderment. What if her feet did get wet? In rainy weather, weren't everyone's feet wet? Why would she need a new pair when she already had shoes without a hole in them?

The day raced by, and before Rose knew it the evening meal was again finished. This time she didn't have Lucy to depend upon, but it wasn't quite so bad because she sat with Cora Mae, another twelve-year-old from her own group. Cora Mae didn't make jokes about everything the way Lucy did, but she was pleasant and friendly. She didn't know anyone at the school, either. Miss Fox had assigned them as partners when she gathered up her group that morning, and Cora Mae and Rose had stayed together ever since.

"They're going to have Store Hour right after we eat," Cora Mae announced.

"What's Store Hour?"

"Like the trading post, I think. I hope so. I like the trading post, don't you?"

"Yes," agreed Rose, remembering the glass counter filled with candy at Goose Hollow. "I don't have anything to trade, though."

"Neither do I," said Cora Mae cheerfully. "My father said he might send me some money later on. He spent all he had to buy me school clothes before I came. But I think we ought to go, even if we haven't any money, don't you? We can see what it's like."

"Yes," agreed Rose quickly. Grandmother would never be able to send her any money, even if she thought of such a thing. She herself would never be able to patronize the trading post at the school, so it was better to go this time when Cora Mae, too, was without money. It wouldn't be hard at all if neither of them could buy anything.

The store was a white, one-storied building on the edge of the campus. It was not connected with the school, except by its location, and students were allowed to patronize it only at specified hours. As Cora Mae had said, it was not too unlike the trading posts at home, except that articles were not taken in trade, and this store sold only things to eat. It had glass counters filled with candy, stacked boxes, containing soft drinks, waxed bags of potato chips and peanuts, and covered vats of ice cream. Moreover, there was no bargaining for commodities. The customer stated his wants, was served, and paid the price asked without argument.

The room was not small, but two minutes after the official time when the children might enter it was crowded. They lined the long counters three deep, and those who had no money to spend stood back in clustered groups, laughing and talking with each other. Store Hour was like a club, a social gathering, and everyone attended.

Cora Mae and Rose occupied a little space by one of the windows. They were tense with the excitement of the occasion, and their eyes took in every detail. They didn't need to buy today. It was enough to be here, a part of the crowd.

After a time, Cora Mae jabbed Rose in the ribs with her elbow.

"Look at that girl," she whispered. "She's in our group. I recognized her. That is the third bottle of pop I have seen her drink since we came. And she was here first, so there's no telling how many she had before that."

Rose looked where Cora Mae pointed. Isobel was standing all alone while the others milled about her. She was drinking strawberry pop into which she had emptied a bag of salted peanuts. It was a combination much favored by the Navahos, and the storekeeper stocked thirty cases of nuts each week to supply the demand. Every time Isobel tilted the bottle, great gulps of it filled her mouth. Occasionally someone jostled against her, but she stood stiff and unyielding, as though she had braced herself against such things. She was not entering into the spirit of the festivities. Her face was expressionless and unsmiling, and she looked neither to left nor right.

"I live in the same room with her," confessed Rose, her dislike for Isobel growing even more.

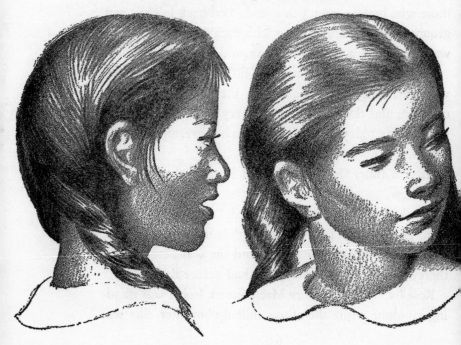

"Oh," said Cora Mae thoughtfully. "She does not look very friendly."

Store Hour came to a close, and again everyone flocked back to the dormitories. It had been an exciting day and an exhausting one. But when the lights were put out Rose did not fall asleep so quickly as she had the night before. She kept thinking of Grandmother, and that hard little lump, which she had never known before leaving home, worked its way up into her throat.

After a certain amount of giggling the twins quieted down, but in the bed below her Rose could hear Isobel turning over and over as though she, too, were having trouble falling asleep. Small wonder, Rose thought disdainfully, the way she made a pig of herself over that pop! It will probably keep her awake for hours, and it serves her right.

71

Classes started the next morning and were not what Rose had been expecting at all. She had been dreading this most important part of school, because she was afraid she wouldn't be able to keep up with the others. What if they learned rapidly, and she was not able to master the strange lessons at all? What if she proved stupid and unable to learn? Then people would be sorry for her all over again, and she had not met pity from anyone since leaving Tuba City. Only the Yuccas knew she had no family, and she had caught only brief glimpses of them since she arrived.

To her delight she found that she could learn as fast as anyone in the room. Some of the children already had a smattering of English. A few, like Isobel, had even attended some day school and were ahead of her. But after that first session she knew she could catch up if she wanted to. And she did want to. She wanted more than anything to excel in something. People couldn't be sorry for someone who was head of the class.

"You can go along in this school as fast as you are able,

72

boys and girls," explained Miss Fox. "We never hold any-one back for the rest of the class."

The teacher was a white lady named Mrs. Hughes. Whatever she said to them was translated into Navaho by Miss Fox, and the first day's lesson consisted in learning the names of things in the room. They learned to say desk, pencil, eraser, blackboard, boy, girl, book, and so on. Some of the children had to repeat the individual names several times because they did not get them right, but Rose listened carefully, pronounced slowly, and each time her effort brought a nod of approval from Mrs. Hughes and her assistant. The only criticism was that Rose, along with the others, did not speak loudly enough.

"White people speak more loudly than we do," explained Miss Fox. "Our voices are low, and we are taught to keep them that way. But when we speak in English, we must raise our voices so that everyone in the room can hear what we say. That is hard to remember. I know, for it was hard for me when I learned to speak English. But it can be done."

In the afternoon Miss Fox took the whole class on a trip to see the school bank and explained it to them.

They marched two by two from their classroom to the room which housed the bank, and at first they were a little disappointed. The bank was only an enclosed stall with a window and counter in front and a door in the back to admit the banker, one of the older boys. Then he showed them a bankbook, and when Miss Fox explained about it they weren't disappointed at all. The bank was exactly like those in cities which were used by white people. Students could put money in the bank, and it would be kept safe for them. No one could steal it. Everyone knew they had money, too, for there was the bankbook to prove it. Whenever they wanted to spend a little, a nickel or a dime, they wrote that amount on a check and signed their names. The banker paid them and saved the rest until they needed it.

"It is a good thing to have money in the bank, boys and girls," said Miss Fox seriously. "With money, you can buy the things you need, and with money in the bank you will be independent. People respect those who have money in the bank."

Rose thought about it eagerly. Here was another way in which she might excel and escape pity. Perhaps if she were rich enough, if she had enough money in the bank, people might overlook her lack of family. They wouldn't be sorry for her and Grandmother. They would envy them. But how could she get money to put in the bank? She discussed the matter with Cora Mae.

"My mother said she would send me some when she next sells her wool," said Cora Mae. "I will have to wait, for sheep cannot be sheared now with winter coming on. But my father may have some money before that, and he may send me some. Perhaps your father will send you some if you ask."

"My father is dead," confessed Rose absently, and then

could have bitten her tongue. She did not want pity.

"That is too bad," sympathized Cora Mae. "But your mother. Has she sheep? Could she send you some money for the bank?"

"My grandmother has more sheep," said Rose evasively. It was perfectly true. She wasn't telling a lie. She just wasn't telling all the truth.

"Then she's sure to send you money," decided Cora Mae promptly. "And an aunt or uncle may send you some too. You can never tell about those things."

"No," agreed Rose soberly. "You can never tell."

The prospects of earning some money of her own did not occur to her. When Miss Fox made the announcement in class the next day she could hardly believe her good fortune.

"In this section of the country, certain crops are grown which we do not raise at home," began Miss Fox. "The farmers who raise these crops grow more than they can pick themselves. They hire other people, and pay them money, to gather their fruits and vegetables. One of these crops is prunes. The prunes are ripe now, and there are not enough pickers to gather them.

"Tomorrow is Saturday, and there will be no school. Any one of you who wants to pick prunes for the farmer may do so. You do not have to unless you want to. If you do want to, you will be paid twenty-five cents for each bushel box of prunes you pick, and the money is yours to keep and to do with as you please. Special busses will leave the school for the orchard at six o'clock in the morning. Lunches will be packed for those who go, and the busses will not return until five in the afternoon. Picking prunes is hard work, and you will get tired. It is up to you to decide whether you want to make extra money."

The announcement was greeted with loud enthusiasm from almost everyone in the class. Navahos are taught from infancy that industry is one of the greatest virtues, and the prospect of earning spending money of their own was something new to these first-year students.

"We can buy all the pop we want at Store Hour," gloated Cora Mae, leaning over toward Rose. "We won't have to stand and watch the others drink it now."

"I am going to buy a red silk scarf to wear around my neck," announced Dolores in a loud whisper. "That's what I will do with my money."

Mrs. Hughes laughed as she rapped on her desk with a ruler, and everyone was instantly quiet. It was time now to start their lessons. They must not waste time, for everything must be learned in five years.

The day passed quickly, as did most days at the school. Almost everyone was anxious to work and make money. At Store Hour and in the Recreation Hall they talked of nothing else. They had been told to wear their oldest clothes, but since Rose had only two dresses and one pair of shoes she had little choice. Cora Mae's clothes had been furnished by her own family, but she didn't have many more.

"Maybe we should buy another dress with our money," Cora Mae worried the next morning, as they stood with the others waiting for the busses to take them to the orchards.

"What for?" asked Rose practically. "We always have one to wear while the other is being washed."

"The older girls have more," pointed out Cora Mae. "In the summer, when they return from school, everyone calls to see what new clothes they have brought home. It makes the family very proud. What would you say to your aunts and uncles and cousins if you returned with nothing new? You would be ashamed."

"I hadn't thought of that," admitted Rose weakly.

She was glad that the busses arrived at that moment, and she and Cora Mae crowded on with the others.

Prune picking was not nearly so hard as Miss Fox had led them to believe. True, they had to sort the prunes as they gathered them up from the ground, to make sure that only hard, firm fruit went into the boxes, but the containers filled up remarkably fast. By quitting time, both Rose and Cora Mae had gathered up twenty bushels. When they turned in their tickets, the overseer gave them fresh new five-dollar bills, which was more money than Rose had ever seen before.

"But I don't know if we'll ever get our clothes clean," mourned Cora Mae. "My dress will wash, but just look at my new shoes."

The prunes had been shaken from the trees, and the

pickers had crawled on their hands and knees to gather them up under each tree. Luckily the ground was dry, but their dresses were spotted and dirty and their shoes were caked with mashed prunes and dirt, and scarred with scuff marks.

"We'll clean them too," insisted Rose stoutly. "I think most of it will wash off."

Most of it did, but the scuffed places in the leather remained and the shoes would never look new again. The girls were almost too tired to care, for by this time fatigue and aching muscles had caught up with them.

"I'm not sure I even want to go to Store Hour," confessed Rose wearily. "I'd just like to go to bed."

"Oh, we can't miss Store Hour," protested Cora Mae. "It's the first time we've had money to buy pop."

As usual there was no room at the counter, but the customers were not nearly so exuberant tonight. There was not so much talking and joking, and those who had already made purchases ate their candy and drank their pop quietly. Weariness showed on most faces, and little groups gathered for only a few moments, then drifted away to the dormitories where there were more comfortable chairs.

"Come on," urged Cora Mae, pulling Rose to the end of the line. She held her five-dollar bill unfolded, so that anyone who was interested could see that she had money.

79

Rose obediently took the place behind Cora Mae. It was tedious waiting in line, especially when the muscles in her legs ached. Her feet felt heavy and too large for her shoes.

She looked at Johnny Paul and Tom Beaver, who had already been served. As she watched, Johnny Paul took a small sip from the half-emptied bottle in his hand. His expression did not change as he put it down. He just stood there, drinking it because he had bought it, but not enjoying it at all.

"Cora Mae." Rose tapped her friend firmly on the shoulder. "Let's get out of line."

Cora Mae turned and stared at her in amazement.

"But we're almost at the front. There are only two people ahead of us."

"I don't want any pop," explained Rose quickly. "Not tonight. I'm too tired. It would just be wasted when I'm so tired."

"But we've waited so long," objected Cora Mae. "All week we've watched the others. And now we have money."

"You stay in line if you want to. I'll wait for you while you drink your pop. But I don't want any tonight."

Cora Mae grumbled a little, and when she rejoined Rose with her bottle of lemon soda she made a great to-do about drinking it. She smacked her lips to show how good it was and kept looking at Rose, hoping to inspire a little envy.

Rose didn't feel envious at all. She held tightly to her five-dollar bill and kept wishing that Cora Mae would finish so she could go to her room and get into bed.

CHAPTER EIGHT

A night's sleep revived everyone, and it was a cheerful crowd that gathered for Sunday breakfast. They felt proud when they remembered how hard they had worked yesterday. Moreover, they felt rich. And today held something special, for they had been invited to attend something called a State Fair. The new students had no idea what a State Fair could be, but the older ones were excited and some of their enthusiasm was contagious.

After breakfast there was church. Attendance was encouraged at the school but was not compulsory. The three sects most prominent on the reservation, Catholic, Protestant, and Latter-day Saints, held services for the children. Most of the older boys and girls were attending one of the services regularly by this time, but some of the new students held back. Rose was one of these. She felt a little guilty when she refused Miss Fox's invitation, but Miss Fox seemed to understand.

"When you are ready let me know," she smiled. "God does not want people to enter His house unwillingly. He will wait."

Rose was glad that God, like Miss Fox, understood. In

the week she had been here, there had been much that was new and strange. When she stopped to remember all of it she felt lost and bewildered, and to try to grasp a new religion at this time was more than she could contemplate. As it was, she felt uneasy enough about the scheduled State Fair.

Again they went by bus. Rose had long since come to the conclusion that everything connected with the white man's world was arrived at by means of busses. They had come to Chemawa on busses. They had used them to travel to and from the prune orchards. She had seen some of the older children depart for town on a bus. Now they were to use busses to reach the State Fair.

She and Cora Mae clambered on, trying to cling to each other's hands so they would not be separated. Almost everyone else was doing the same thing, for there was safety in numbers, and partners for the fair had been arranged long ago.

It was only a short ride to the place of the State Fair. They drove through a gate, and the driver leaned out his window and called "Chemawa" to the guard, who stood back and waved them on. Inside there was nothing to be seen but parked cars. Old cars, new ones, large and small cars, cars with sparkling new paint and cars with no paint at all. They stood in neat lines, one after another in the fields on either side of the road. Rose hadn't known there were so many cars in the world, and neither had Cora Mae. They discussed this amazing thing in low voices, especially when they discovered there were even more cars coming, all of which turned into the parking areas and lined themselves up alongside the others. The busses turned off after a while and backed and turned into spaces that looked far too small but which somehow fitted the length and width of the bus exactly.

The teacher-interpreters got out first, and their groups collected around them.

"Are we all here?" asked Miss Fox brightly. Her eyes were shining with pleasure, and Rose decided a State Fair couldn't be so very terrifying since Miss Fox was looking forward to it. "Stay with me, boys and girls. Try to keep together at all times. I don't want anyone to lag behind and get lost."

Through the turnstile they went, and the ticket taker stood back to let them through without paying. The students of Chemawa were guests of the fair this afternoon.

Rose clung tightly to Cora Mae's hand, her eyes growing wider by the minute as they marched along. There were big buildings filled with displays, giant fruit and vegetables, grain and flowers. There were canned foods in crystal-clear jars, and baked delicacies. There were handiwork displays, quilts and lace-trimmed linens, clothing of every kind, weaving, knitting, beadwork, embroidery. After this they went into other buildings, some of which contained strange and intricate machinery, others livestock. Rose gazed at row after row of cattle,

horses, pigs, and sheep. The latter made her a little home-sick, and she reached over and let her fingers trail through the thick, soft fleece. It was comforting in its familiarity, but strange, too, for their own sheep never grew wool so thick and long. What blankets and rugs could be woven from the fleece of these animals!

It took a long time to see everything. Their feet got very tired, their throats became dry, especially after they had breathed the dusty, straw-scented air of the barns, and their eyes grew heavy with looking at so much.

"There's just time for a quick tour of the carnival block," announced Miss Fox finally. "We're to meet at the bus at five o'clock, and it's four-thirty now. This way, boys and girls."

The carnival block was the most enchanting place of all. They heard the excited screams and laughter of happy people long before they reached there. They smelled it before then, too, for the fragrance of frying pronto pups and hamburgers, of mustard, popcorn, and peanuts carried a long way on the warm September air. They rounded the corner of a building and there it was, the carnival block, gay and colorful and exciting.

Rose thought she had never seen such a place. There was a big wheel with hanging seats, which went around and around in the air, and a twisting, writhing vehicle which went up and down and around and around, bumping over tracks and jerking the occupants of the seats so that their heads seemed about to snap off. Rose couldn't understand why they seemed to be enjoying that ride, for it certainly couldn't be comfortable. There were gayly painted horses which galloped in a circle to the strains of sparkling music. There were stands with tantalizing articles on display, golden vases, stuffed animals, dishes, dolls with bright feathered skirts, clocks, and pennants. These were to be won, it was decided, by feats of skill.

"Can we try, Miss Fox?" demanded Johnny Paul eagerly.

"Can we ride on the bouncy thing that goes up and down?" cried Tom Beaver.

Miss Fox looked sad.

"Those things cost money," she explained. "You have to pay to ride and pay to play the games. The school hasn't money for that. The fair let us in free, or we wouldn't be here at all."

"I have some money," cried Johnny Paul, feeling in the pocket of his heavy blue jeans. "I brought some with me. May I try, Miss Fox?"

"If that's the way you want to spend the money you worked so hard to earn."

Johnny Paul gave a whoop of delight and started on a run toward one of the bright stands. Miss Fox and the other children followed to see Johnny win a prize.

"I'm going to take that big horse made of gold," he told the man, but because he spoke in Navaho the man only shrugged his shoulders and looked blank.

Miss Fox spoke to the man in English, then translated for the children.

"To win the large horse you must throw nine balls into the bottle," she explained. "The balls cost three for twenty-five cents. Even if you managed to get every ball into the bottle, that would cost seventy-five cents. And you may not win. If it were easy to do, I doubt if they would stay in business long."

"I can do it," insisted Johnny eagerly. "I don't think it will be hard."

He pulled a badly crumpled dollar bill from his pocket. The man handed him a quarter in change and placed a row of small white balls in front of him. Johnny Paul smiled widely. He selected one of the balls, drew back, and took aim. The ball whizzed across the open space and rolled out of sight behind one of the shelves. It did not come near the bottle.

The next time Johnny Paul did not take such a wide swing. He leaned over the counter and tossed the ball gently. It fell short of the bottle, and so did the third shot.

The young Navahos were laughing loudly. It was a great joke to see Johnny Paul try and miss. Rose didn't laugh. She was remembering all the prunes Johnny Paul had gathered on his hands and knees before he had money to pay for the three balls.

The fourth ball managed to go into the bottle, and everyone cheered. It wasn't funny now. Johnny Paul was one of theirs, and they were proud of this shot. But the next ball, and the next, went wild. By the time Johnny Paul had used up the nine balls only two of them had gone inside the bottle.

Johnny wanted to buy more chances, but Miss Fox said no. They must walk on and look at other things, and Johnny couldn't remain behind. He looked very sad and crestfallen as he shuffled along, now and then glancing at the ugly glass dish which had been his prize for tossing two balls into the bottle.

Two or three of the children ventured a turn on one of the dazzling rides, but most of them had left their earnings from prune picking at school and could only stand and watch. How could they have known that the State

Fair would present such a temptation to spend money?

Rose was not one of these. In the pocket of her coat she carried her five-dollar bill, mainly because she could not bear to leave it behind. It was the first money she had ever owned, and she had slept with it beneath her pillow last night. Cora Mae had not been so provident.

"Oh, I wish I had brought my money," she mourned. "Just a little of it. I'd give anything to ride on that big wheel."

Rose wanted to ride on the big wheel too. She wanted to soar up and up into the sky. At the top I could look down the way a bird does, she thought. I could imagine I was an eagle and see the world as it looks to him. What a thing to tell Grandmother when I got home!

She was just opening her mouth to tell Cora Mae that she would pay for the two of them to ride in the big wheel when Miss Fox announced it was time to go.

"We have only ten minutes to walk back to the bus," she said. "We'll have to step right along, too. It's quite a ways."

The ride back to Chemawa was a noisy one. There was no end to the things they had to talk about. Did you see this? Do you remember that? If we ever get to go to a State Fair again—— Conversations bubbled on both sides of the aisle, and the bus driver, catching one of the teacher's glances, grinned and shook his head helplessly. Only Rose had little to say. She listened with half an ear while Cora Mae rattled on, but she was really thinking how filled was the world with temptations. There was Store Hour, with its displays of pop and candy. There were clothes which one ought to buy if one expected to have the admiration of others. There were such things as the State Fair, and in this new life so filled with surprises tomorrow might bring something else. The next time she was confronted with a temptation she might not be so strong.

They arrived at the school, and the bus began to disgorge passengers. It was suppertime. They suddenly remembered they were hungry, and everyone wanted to get to the cafeteria at once.

"Come on," called Cora Mae impatiently, but Rose shook her head. She had to find Miss Fox. She must find her immediately before another temptation presented itself.

Miss Fox was hungry, too, but she obligingly turned to wait when she heard her name being called.

"Here," said Rose quickly, holding out the precious five-dollar bill. It was limp and bedraggled from much folding. "Take it, please. I want you to take it. It's for money in the bank."

CHAPTER NINE

After the weekend of the fair, school settled down to a regular routine. The six o'clock wake-up bell was unnecessary, for by that time the Navahos had long been out of their beds. Their washing and ironing were neatly finished and their rooms immaculately cleaned. After breakfast there were certain chores. Halls must be swept and living rooms dusted, for there was no money to pay for the services of a dormitory janitor, and the children themselves kept the building clean. In addition, the new students had discovered that there were extra, harder jobs which could be voluntarily assumed, for which the school paid in clothing. Rose had already started working for a flowered skirt like Miss Fox's. Eventually her two dresses would wear out, and she must be prepared. Half and quarter hours of work were duly credited on a chart, to be totaled up to the necessary amount.

Classwork occupied most of the day, with a break for the noon meal. In the afternoon there were more classes, which included shop for the boys and home economics for the girls, and before they knew it, it was four o'clock and Store Hour. Everybody went to Store Hour, whether he had money to spend or not. After supper there was the Recreation Hall, with often some additional studying to be done before it was time to wash and go to bed.

Saturdays were full too. Prunes had been followed by the nut harvest, and almost the whole student body set out on weekends to gather walnuts or filberts for the neighboring farmers. Rose's bankbook now showed almost fourteen dollars credited to her account.

She always fell asleep quickly once she climbed into her bed, but one night she was awakened with a start. The room was enshrouded in thick blackness, and because there was no moon the open window was a square of dark gray, only a little lighter in shade.

She had been aroused by a sound, a strange muffled sound which seemed to come from far away, and at first she clutched the bedclothes tightly, almost afraid to breathe. It could very well be the ghost of an earth person, for everyone knows that ghosts appear only after darkness, and on moonless nights. Then she realized it wasn't the mourning voice of a ghost, for the sound was not from outside. It was in the room, and it came from the bed below her own. Isobel was making that strange muffled noise. She was crying.

Rose leaned over the edge of the bunk.

"Isobel!" she whispered. "Isobel, what's the matter?"

Isobel did not answer, but for a moment the crying stopped. Then it started again, as though it was beyond her control.

Rose swung her feet over the edge and slipped to the floor. It would be just as well not to awaken the peacefully sleeping twins. She sat on the edge of Isobel's bed and reached over to pat the shaking shoulders.

"Isobel, has a sickness taken hold of you? Shall I call the matron?"

Isobel's whole body shook in protest. It announced that she was not sick. She didn't want the matron.

Rose didn't feel that the matron would do much good either. If Isobel had contracted sickness or disease it was because she had violated a taboo or had been attacked by a ghost or a witch. If the latter was the case and the spectral attack was very recent it could be averted or lessened by certain precautions.

She fumbled her way through the darkness to the dresser. Her fingers slipped down, counting, until they arrived at her own drawer. Inside, carefully laid away with her change of underwear and her sweater, was a tiny sack of gall medicine. Grandmother had made it for her just before she left home, so it was fresh and potent. It was composed of dried and pulverized galls of many animals and was a sure cure for anyone who had unknowingly absorbed a witch's poison.

"Get up, Isobel," Rose insisted in a firm whisper. "You've got to come with me."

The bed once more shook with Isobel's refusal.

Rose pulled back the blankets firmly, holding them there despite Isobel's fumbling attempts to jerk them back. One of the twins moved restlessly and mumbled something in her sleep.

"If you don't come, I'll wake Dolores and Maria. Three of us can drag you," whispered Rose fiercely.

Isobel got out of bed. Her crying was not so violent as before, but her sturdy body shook with an occasional racking sob. Rose took her by the hand, guiding her out of the room. A dim light was kept burning at night in the long corridor, and Isobel's face appeared red and puffy. She must have been crying a long time before I heard her, Rose told herself anxiously. She hoped it was not too late for the gall medicine to take effect. There was only one cure for the poison of a witch or a ghost, once it had really taken hold, and that was to have the Enemy Way sung over the victim. No one here would know or be qualified to perform such a ceremonial.

She pulled Isobel into the deserted bathroom, switched on the light, and closed the door firmly behind them. Fortunately someone had left a water glass on the shelf, and she filled it at the tap, dumping in a generous sprinkling of gall medicine from the bag. She knew it should be boiled a long while to produce the necessary qualities of an emetic, but there was no time for that. Isobel's swollen red face showed she was already too far gone to wait.

"Drink it," she ordered sternly, holding out the glass.

Isobel accepted it meekly. Tonight she had lost all of her former disdainful manner. She looked very forlorn and pitiful. Her shoulders, in the outing-flannel sleeves of her pajamas, sagged mournfully, and already she seemed to be coming down with a chill.

"It's gall medicine," explained Rose. "My grandmother made it for me. Drink it fast."

Isobel obeyed. The water, choked with shriveled brown fragments, disappeared down her throat. She shuddered a little, gulped, and held out the empty glass.

"You'll feel better soon," promised Rose, trying to make her voice carry an assurance she did not feel. "We'll go back to bed soon, and in the morning you'll feel fine."

"No," said Isobel in a choked voice. "I won't. I know I won't."

But she had stopped crying, which was a good sign. Perhaps it was not too late for the gall medicine to work after all. Rose waited, while they both shivered with cold, for the emetic to take effect. Nothing happened, and finally they gave up. There was no use waiting any longer.

They tiptoed back down the murky corridor and into their own room where the twins continued to sleep peacefully. Isobel climbed into bed, and, without thinking, Rose leaned over and tucked the blankets around her. Grandmother always tucked the sheepskins around Rose when she was sad or upset, and it seemed a natural thing to do. In the darkness she heard Isobel catch her breath. There was a little pause before she whispered a weak good night.

"Good night," answered Rose. She tried very hard to

sound bright and reassuring. "I'll see you in the morning."

In the morning, however, Isobel was not in her bed. She must have got up and dressed while it was still night. Her pajamas were thrown on the floor, and most amazing of all, the bed itself was tumbled and unmade.

"Where's Isobel?" demanded Dolores.

"She probably went down the hall," answered Maria carelessly.

Rose said nothing, but she was troubled about their roommate's absence. After she had finished making her own bed, she made Isobel's, and hung the two pairs of pajamas in the closet. The gall medicine had been taken too late. Isobel's body was already filled with the witch's poison. But where was she? Even though ill and filled with poison she still had to be somewhere.

There was no sign of her at breakfast, nor did she appear in the classroom when school took up. Mrs. Hughes called the roll, and each pupil except Isobel answered "present" to his name.

"Is Isobel sick?" asked Mrs. Hughes of Miss Fox.

Miss Fox shook her head and inquired of the class.

"Do any of you girls know what has happened to Isobel?"

Everyone looked blank, and after a moment Rose put up her hand. She couldn't keep the secret any longer. Isobel must be found and sent home. She must return to the reservation so that the proper singers could perform the Enemy Way ceremonial.

"May I speak to you, Miss Fox? May I speak to you alone?"

Miss Fox looked startled and said something to Mrs. Hughes. Then she beckoned Rose to follow her out of the room and into the hall.

"Tell me what has happened," she insisted as the door closed behind them.

Rose told the whole story of waking up and discovering there was no moon, of hearing Isobel's sobs, and her own realization that a ghost or a witch was abroad in the night. She told of the gall medicine, and how it hadn't worked properly because it hadn't been boiled, and how in the morning she had discovered that Isobel had been spirited away.

Miss Fox listened carefully to everything.

"Rose," she said finally. "It was not a witch or a ghost who poisoned Isobel. There are no ghosts or witches here. Isobel is sick from something else. She is sick with loneliness."

"With loneliness?"

"She has never been away from home before," nodded Miss Fox. "I know that the rest of you haven't either, but people are made differently inside. They have different feelings and express those feelings differently. You have had moments of homesickness when you thought of your family and wished you were with them. But those moments passed because you have made other friends and have found things to occupy your mind. You have kept busy and are adjusting to your surroundings. I have watched Isobel for some time, and I've been worried about her. She doesn't seem to have any special friends. I always see her alone."

"She doesn't want to make friends, Miss Fox."

"How do you know she doesn't? Did she tell you so?"

"No, but she doesn't act friendly. She acts as though she thought she was better than anyone else. She never says anything to anybody. I know she doesn't, because she lives in the same room with me. She doesn't talk. She doesn't even look at us very much. She wants to be by herself."

"Do you know what it is to be shy, Rose?"

Shy? She, who once was called Sad Girl because she kept to herself and never smiled? Rose almost laughed aloud, but Miss Fox was looking too serious to dare such a thing.

"She isn't shy, Miss Fox. Why should she be shy? What does she have to be shy about?"

"I don't know that any more than you do. But I know she is. Think back, Rose. You say that Isobel has never given any sign that she wanted to be friends. Have you ever given her a sign that you'd like to be her friend?"

Rose hung her head. There was much in what Miss Fox said. The friends she herself had made since leaving home had all of them given her to understand they were willing to be friendly. There was Lucy on the bus, Miss Fox and the teachers, Cora Mae and many of the boys and girls in her class. There was Mary Yucca at home. Grace and Tony would have been friendly if only she had let them.

She realized suddenly that it had always been the other person who gave the first signal of friendship, the smile, the word or gesture. She herself had never volunteered such a thing. She didn't exactly know how to go about it. Perhaps Isobel didn't know either.

"I'm going to explain things to Mrs. Hughes, then I'm going to look for Isobel." Miss Fox was watching her closely. "You may return to class, Rose, or you may be excused to go with me. It's up to you to decide."

"I'll go with you to find Isobel."

Miss Fox smiled, showing both dimples. She went back to speak with Mrs. Hughes, and Rose waited in the hall. She tried to think where they should look first. Isobel couldn't be in their own dormitory. Someone had been in every part of that earlier in the morning. Unless Isobel had played hide-and-seek she would have been discovered before this. The same thing was true of the other dormitories, the classrooms and administration buildings. She must be outside.

Rose closed her eyes to think better. The grounds at Chemawa were quite open, and for some reason she doubted if Isobel would be hiding in the shrubbery. Probably she had gone off the grounds. She might be walking home along the highway, or perhaps she had wandered onto one of the neighboring farms. A farm! That was it. Some place that smelled faintly of home, where there was no one around, and where she could imagine she was back in her native Utah.

"Gracious," said Miss Fox in dismay when Rose told her of her conclusions. "You may be right, but that covers a lot of territory. There are acres of farm lands adjoining the school property."

"But I think I know where to look," insisted Rose eagerly. "The day we went to the State Fair we saw one place where there were sheep. We saw them from the bus windows. Everyone spoke of them. It was like seeing home, and we wished they were closer to the road. I think if I were Isobel and homesick I would remember the sheep and go there."

"Very well," agreed Miss Fox. "We'll look there first. Show me the place of the sheep."

The scents of fall were beginning to fill the air, and its colors marked the countryside with splotches of yellow and red. Someone was burning trash, and a tinge of smoke hung low over the fields. The sky had lost its vivid summer shade and looked faded. Blue always did that eventually, Rose told herself. She remembered a bolt of bright blue velveteen on the trader's shelf at Goose Hollow. Everyone admired it, but no one could afford to buy it. They chose scarlets and crimsons when they were buying material for new blouses. Reds would keep their colors through many years, but under the blazing reservation sun a blue would soon fade to light, then an ugly gray. It would take a very rich woman indeed to afford a sky-colored blouse which would soon lose its color.

They walked down the gravel road which led to the highway, and Rose pointed out the field where they had glimpsed the sheep.

"There were only a few," she remembered, "and it is not a large field. Perhaps by now they have moved on to another pasture."

"We'll look, anyway," decided Miss Fox. She left the road and struck off across the rough, grassy field. "There's a fence line over there. They keep sheep fenced in this part of the country. If they're still pastured here it will be in an enclosure."

Rose thought how strange it was to fence grazing land. Sheep took a lot of pasture. They had to wander miles in order to find forage. Then she looked at the countryside through which they were walking and realized that what held true at home was not so in this place. Here the grass grew thick, covering the soil completely—not in scattered clumps. The duties of a herder would be small, for there was no sagebrush to make the greedy sheep puff up should they eat it, no locoweed to make them run in senseless circles. She wondered what white children did to occupy their time since they were not needed to tend the flocks.

They reached the fence, and Miss Fox parted the strands of wire, holding up the top which was barbed with sharp spikes. Rose climbed through, then held it for Miss Fox. They were in the field where the sheep had been, but there was no sign of them now.

"We'll walk a little way farther," decided Miss Fox. "If you remember this place, Isobel may remember it too."

A hundred yards on they found her. Isobel was sitting on the ground as she had so often sat on her own bed in the dormitory, her hands clasped on her lap, her knees folded under her. She had been screened from sight by the slope of the land, but when she saw them coming she made no move to run away. She did not speak or wave a greeting, and her face wore an expression of hopelessness.

Miss Fox said nothing either. She sat on the ground beside Isobel, and after a moment Rose sat on the other side. For a long time they were silent, and Rose felt a sense of companionship gradually come over her. It was the same feeling she and Grandmother had often shared at night in the hogan. They said nothing, but after a while it seemed that speech was unnecessary, for their thoughts were shared without words.

"It is good to sit here," said Isobel after a long time. "There has been no one around me but the Holy People. Changing Woman, the earth, is preparing for her old age which comes with the winter. I do not think she minds that she must grow old for a time, for she knows she will be young again in the spring. I saw Dawn Boy in the sky early this morning, and now Sun, the husband of Changing Woman, smiles at me. Gila Monster also knows I am here, for he has sent some soft winds from the south to blow upon me."

"It is good to be with old friends," said Miss Fox softly. "But new friends are good too."

"I have no new friends." Isobel's voice was steady. Her tears had run dry the night before. "This is not a good place for me. There is no happiness here. The others here do not like me, but at home I am liked. I have many friends at home. It is better that I go home, Miss Fox. I should not have come."

"Isobel, you're wrong. You do have friends here. I am your friend," cried Rose. She found that she was telling the truth. This was a new Isobel who sat beside her on the grass. This one wasn't proud and disdainful at all. Even her turquoise and silver jewelry meant nothing today. They represented the "hard" wealth of a Navaho, but one can have more than his share of "hard" wealth and still be poor. He is poor if he is without songs and stories and without friends.

Isobel turned and looked at her steadily after Rose spoke, and then she smiled a little wistfully. Rose realized with surprise that Isobel was pretty when she smiled. It made her seem a different person altogether.

"Thank you," she said gravely. "You are kind. You tried to be kind last night. You are kind today. But I must go home."

"It will be different if you stay," pleaded Rose. "You don't know how different it will be. You'll have many friends. I'll ask Mrs. Hughes if you can change your seat to be by Cora Mae and me. You'll have your meals with us. And when the twins laugh and giggle with each other, you and I can share a little joke of our own."

Isobel looked doubtful.

"Will you try it for a week?" asked Miss Fox. "Will you give the school one more chance? I promise you that if you're still homesick after another week I'll help you go back home."

"I will try," agreed Isobel after another silence. "My

family wanted me to come here, and I wanted to come. But they would want me to be happy."

"You will be happy," promised Rose quickly. "You're going to be very happy."

She got to her feet and reached a hand to help pull Isobel to hers. Isobel looked surprised and smiled shyly as she accepted the offer. Somehow, as the three of them retraced their steps across the field, they found they were still clinging to each other's hands.

CHAPTER TEN

"I suppose we have to go to this thing Miss Fox calls a movie," said Rose a little doubtfully. "At least we must go once to please her."

"We can always shut our eyes if we don't like it," giggled Maria, polishing away at the mirror. Since it was Saturday, their room was having its weekly thorough cleaning.

"You will like it. You won't shut your eyes," said Isobel timidly.

Rose turned and beamed at her proudly. She was determined to draw Isobel out and include her in things, but Isobel was shy. It was not often that she expressed a definite opinion like this, although she had stopped insisting that she must return home.

"How do you know?" asked Dolores curiously.

"Because I saw a movie once."

"What was it like? Was it the way Miss Fox said it was? Is it really pictures, and do the pictures really speak and move?"

"Yes, only they speak in English, so I could not understand them."

"Tell us about it. Was there anything else that Miss Fox left out?"

Isobel shook her head and began plumping a pillow hard to hide her embarrassment. She could think of nothing to add, nothing at all.

"I'm glad you're going with us," said Rose. "With Cora Mae and me. We've never seen a movie. You can tell us about it as we go along."

The weekly movies were getting a late start this year, but now that they had begun they would be shown on each Saturday night for the remainder of school. The older students were looking forward to them eagerly, but the first-year groups were a little fearful. People said that movies must be shown in a darkened room, which could be dangerous in itself. There must be something of magic or the supernatural in a picture which talked and moved. There might be other things, too, of which they had not yet heard. What if the older students did laugh at possible danger? Wasn't there always a first time?

As much as they dreaded the new experience, they looked forward to it, too, and the day passed slowly. They finished their rooms and the Saturday chores which had been assigned around the dormitory. They ate lunch, and afterwards some of them ironed or mended clothing while some went to the Recreation Hall.

Rose decided to spend the time with schoolwork. They had just begun writing, and she was not satisfied with the way her own samples looked. They weren't beautifully even like Mrs. Hughes's, and she was sure that practice would make them better. Isobel hadn't seemed able to find anything to do, but she was contented to sit on her bed and watch Rose work.

In the middle of the afternoon Cora Mae appeared at the door. In her hand was a pair of her scissors, on her face an impish smile.

"Guess what," she said to Rose. "I'm going to cut my hair."

"You're what?" Rose put down her pencil, her eyes widening with astonishment. "Oh, Cora Mae! No!"

"Why not? Everybody's doing it this afternoon. There's nothing else to do."

"But Cora Mae, what will your mother say?"

"Not much probably. She may not like it at first, but she will when she gets used to it. And I'm tired of doing braids. Here you have to do them every day. It takes so long. Besides, short hair's much more stylish."

"Yes, I guess it is," agreed Rose slowly. She thought of Miss Fox and the lovely way her short hair had been trained to curl around her face. Most of the older girls had short hair, but she had considered that was something which came with age.

"And we want to be in style, don't we?" demanded Cora Mae. "I tell you, everybody's doing it this afternoon. We don't want to be the only ones with braids. Look at Isobel. Even she's got short hair. It was short when she came."

Isobel did not seem to notice the slighting tone. She shrugged her shoulders and said nothing.

"Then her mother knows about it," pointed out Rose. "She doesn't care, does she, Isobel? Or she wouldn't have let you cut it. But I think my grandmother wouldn't like it if I cut mine."

"Then don't," advised Isobel unexpectedly. "My brother has been to school. He said the girls at his school had short hair, and my mother agreed I would be more comfortable if my hair looked like theirs. Now I do not think it matters, but that is why I cut it before I came."

"Your grandmother will get used to it," urged Cora Mae. "And if she doesn't, it will grow back. Look, I have scissors. We'll cut our hair together. I will cut yours, and you cut mine."

Rose remembered how Grandmother had looked at Grace Yucca's hair. She had not approved and had thought it one of the white man's ways which the Navaho did not need to follow.

"I don't want my hair cut," said Rose flatly. "I don't mind doing the braids."

"You're afraid to," declared Cora Mae.

"What is there to be afraid of?" asked Isobel. "There is no pain to cutting hair."

"She's afraid of what her grandmother might do to her if she cuts it."

"My grandmother would do nothing. She would say nothing, either, although she would not like it," said Rose proudly. "I just don't want it cut."

"Well, I'm going to cut mine," declared Cora Mae huffily. "And if you won't cut it for me I'll find someone who will."

"I'll cut it for you if you want me to," offered Isobel. "I've never cut anyone's hair, but I've watched while it was done."

"Fine," said Cora Mae defiantly, looking at Rose.

She sat in the straight chair, and Isobel pinned a towel around her neck and unloosened the two braids which hung down her back. At this point Cora Mae began to look a little apprehensive.

"Don't cut it too short," she warned.

"Do you want it cut at all?" asked Isobel, pausing with the scissors in her hand.

"Oh yes, cut it. And when Rose sees how stylish I look she'll want hers cut too."

When the first long strand of black hair fell to the floor Cora Mae shut her eyes.

"I can't look," she admitted. "I won't look till you're finished."

Rose watched though, watched as the long black mane was clipped off in a neat straight line a little below the bottom of Cora Mae's ears. Isobel may have had no experience in cutting hair, but her hands were clever and her eye held to a straight line. When she parted some of the hair in front and cut bangs straight across the middle of Cora Mae's forehead it seemed to change her whole

appearance. It was a different girl sitting there with a towel fastened around her neck.

"Oh, Cora Mae, it's beautiful. You look so pretty," exclaimed Rose in admiration.

Cora Mae opened her tightly closed eyes, got up, and crossed the room to the mirror.

"I do look different. I'm not the same person. They'll have to look twice to tell who I am."

"You've done a wonderful job, Isobel," said Rose, including her in the praise. "It's a good thing you were here when Cora Mae wanted her hair cut. I could never have done half so well."

Isobel flushed and smiled.

"Now cut hers," demanded Cora Mae. "Cut Rose's. She wants to look nice, too, now that she sees how easy it is."

"No," said Isobel flatly. "I won't."

"Why not?" asked Cora Mae in surprise. "You would if she wanted you to, wouldn't you?"

"No," said Isobel. "I won't cut her hair. She looks better in braids." She put down the scissors and comb and ended the argument by walking out of the room.

"Stubborn thing," said Cora Mae. "You'd better wait till she changes her mind, Rose. None of the other haircuts I've seen this afternoon are half as good as the one she gave."

The much discussed movie was scheduled for seven o'clock. Anticipation made the evening meal a very gay affair, and the fresh new bobs of the first-year students added to the festivities. All but three or four of the new girls had cut their long hair that afternoon, and there was much tossing of heads and comments about it. What a timesaver it would be! How easy it was to care for! How attractive the style made everyone look!

Rose felt very much out of things. She had nothing to contribute to the conversation, and she began to wish she hadn't been so thoughtful of Grandmother's feelings. There was no denying the fact that the girls looked pretty n their new hair styles, and she herself felt very plain in her usual braids. She was grateful for Isobel, silently eating dinner beside her. Isobel was an outsider, too.

"Do you think they'll ever stop talking about it?" she whispered.

Isobel seemed to know what Rose meant, and her smile was full of sympathy and understanding.

"Just as soon as something else happens that they can talk about," she nodded.

The auditorium began to fill immediately after they left the cafeteria. The movies were free, so the student body attended in full force. They couldn't be the latest releases, for that would have cost too much money, but it didn't matter since they were new to most of the students.

To Rose's delight the auditorium lights were on as they entered. She and Cora Mae and Isobel found seats in the center of the room and settled themselves to wait.

"That's the screen," Isobel told them, pointing to a large white square mounted on a stand in the center of the stage. "The pictures will come on there."

"What are we supposed to do?" demanded Cora Mae, running her fingers through her hair.

"Nothing. Just sit and watch."

The auditorium filled and the doors were closed. Then came the moment which Rose had been dreading. The lights were turned off. The darkness lasted only a minute, however, for the screen on the stage came alive. Lines of writing which she could not read glowed on the screen, while the sounds of an orchestra filled the room

The first sheet of writing was followed by other sheets, this time in smaller type and also unintelligible, then they were replaced by a picture. It was a landscape, rolling and rimrock ledged, and seeing it brought a lump in her throat, for it was like part of home.

Suddenly there appeared a wagon, only it was unlike the wagons she had seen in her lifetime, for this one had a white top, like a tent. It was drawn by horses that actually moved in the picture, pulling the wagon after them. In the wagon seat driving the team was a whiskery white man and seated beside him the most beautiful lady Rose had ever seen. She had dimples, a dazzling smile, and her head was covered with golden curls that cascaded down her back to her waist. They spoke together, these two in the wagon, and while Rose could not understand what they were saying, she was sure they were father and daughter.

Soon they made camp, and before the audience's eyes a house was built. It went up remarkably fast but that was not strange, for these movies were certainly magic. A handsome young man appeared who seemed to be the sweetheart of the beautiful young lady. Unfortunately, he could not stay long in the new house, for he obviously had an errand somewhere. After an affectionate good-by from the young lady, who wept to see him go, he rode away.

Rose wanted at this point to call a warning to the young

lady. As a matter of fact, some of the audience did so, but the young lady did not hear. She did not know she was being spied upon by a scout in breechclout and with a single feather in his hair. Rose looked carefully. He belonged to a tribe she did not know. No Navaho would wear a feather like that. He was a bad man. Soon he stole away, and the movie showed him joining others of his strange tribe. They wore painted stripes upon their faces, and she concluded these must be the war markings of this particular tribe. She had never seen anything like them, even when the old ones danced the war dances of the ancients.

The bad tribe then rode out to attack. They tried to intercept the handsome young man who had rashly chosen this moment to return to the house, but he managed to elude them. He got inside, and he and the father and the beautiful young lady shot at the bad men through windows.

Then one of the bad men thought of setting fire to the house. They fastened a blazing stick to an arrow and shot it onto the roof. Rose marveled that an arrow could carry such a distance. Again it was the magic of movies which made it do so, she concluded. The roof caught fire and began to burn just as the picture changed.

For a moment she was a little dizzy and resentful of the change. How hateful of the movie to leave those three good people in a burning house and show a picture of soldiers riding horses. But the older boys and girls, who could follow the words of the people in the movie, cheered loudly. In another moment Rose herself was cheering. The soldiers were approaching the burning house. The bad men saw them coming and rushed to get away, the soldiers in hot pursuit. Father, the beautiful lady, and the handsome gentleman threw open the door of the burning house and in billows of smoke rushed out into safety.

Then it was over. The lights went on, and Rose realized with a start she was still in the auditorium. She hadn't been there in her thoughts for a long time. She had been with the people in the movie, living a strange, exciting story.

"How did you like it?" asked Isobel softly.

"Oh, it was wonderful. I wish I could see a movie every night."

Others seemed to agree with her. As they poured out of the doors it was all they talked about. Did you see—— Don't you think—— If I'd have been there I'd have——

Isobel, Cora Mae, and Rose started across the campus to McBride Hall, where the younger girls lived. They felt excited and warm, reluctant to leave the enchanted world of the movie.

"I got so interested I almost forgot about my new haircut," confided Cora Mae.

"Oh—hair," said Isobel smoothly. "Didn't that girl in the movie have the most beautiful hair you ever saw?"

"She certainly did," agreed Cora Mae and Rose earnestly.

"So soft and long," continued Isobel. "You know, Rose, if your hair were curled it would look almost like that. It's about as long. Only the color is different, and the color doesn't matter."

"Yes," said Cora Mae in a strange voice. "I guess it is about the length of hers at that."

CHAPTER ELEVEN

Grace Yucca stopped in the path and smiled impartially on Rose, Isobel, and Cora Mae.

"Today I had a letter from my family," she announced. "The trader wrote it for them. They are all in good health, and he says that your grandmother, too, is well."

It was the first time Rose had seen Grace except from a distance and the only conversation they had had since leaving Tuba City. Despite the momentary rush of warmth at the news of Grandmother's well-being she felt herself on guard, wondering if Grace was remembering her as Sad Girl, only granddaughter of She-Who-Knows-Much-Trouble.

"Thank you," she said dutifully, and tugged at Isobel and Cora Mae to make them move on. They, however, stayed where they were. It was not every day that one of the older girls engaged the younger ones in conversation. They were too absorbed in their own activities.

"How are you getting along?" smiled Grace.

"Fine."

"I told you you'd like it once you got used to it," nodded Grace, and walked on.

For a moment Rose wanted to run after her. What else had the letter said? What were people doing around Goose Hollow? Were there any changes? How was Grandmother managing without her? Something held her back, and when the girls started on she went with them.

"Did you notice her jacket?" asked Cora Mae. "She made it in home economics. All the third-year girls made wool jackets for themselves this year. I wish we could make something like that, instead of bedroom slippers and pajamas."

"We will," Isobel assured her. "We have to learn to use the machines better before they'll give us expensive material to practice on."

"I suppose you're right," admitted Cora Mae regretfully. "You usually are."

Isobel had finally made an adjustment to the school, and now she had as many friends as anyone. It hadn't been easy. During the first three months of school, patterns had been formed and the other students had come to regard Isobel as someone who occupied a seat in the classroom, a bed in the dormitory, yet took no part in the school groups.

Rose had deliberately pushed and pulled Isobel into one thing after another. Cora Mae had been a little sulky at first, but she had given in to the idea that they were to be three instead of two. Isobel walked with them to and from class. She sat with them at meals, and Rose saw that she was included in games at the Recreation Hall.

Gradually Isobel had been accepted by the others, and ordinarily Rose was proud to see that Isobel was even making friends on her own initiative. But Rose wasn't thinking of that now. She was thinking of Grandmother at Goose Hollow.

"It's nice to have somebody from home here in school with you," said Isobel. "I haven't anybody. Everyone I know who went away to school went someplace else. I was too late deciding, and that's why I had to come here."

"Me too," nodded Cora Mae. "I hope my family is all right."

"Why don't we write them a letter and ask?" demanded Isobel, her black eyes sparkling. "Mrs. Hughes would help us."

"We can't write well enough," protested Rose quickly. Ever since the bus trip when Lucy Smith had told her about letters she had been worrying about them. It wasn't that she didn't want to send a letter to Grandmother. It would make the old lady very happy and proud to receive a message. But how could she address it so that people would know for whom it was meant? Unless the Yuccas had told her, Grandmother wouldn't know that Rose had adopted a family name for them. The trader wouldn't know, and when a letter came addressed to Smith he wouldn't know what to do with it. Rose could put She-Who-Knows-Much-Trouble on the envelope and people would know, but she didn't want to do that. It was such a sad reminder that it might overshadow the letter.

"We can write some of the words ourselves," insisted Isobel. "And what we haven't learned Miss Fox will show us. I've been meaning to write to my family anyway. They've already written to me."

"They have?" Cora Mae was much impressed.

"My brother wrote," nodded Isobel. "He writes words. He went to school at Intermountain. But the letter he wrote was for all of them, from my mother and father, my grandmother, and all the aunts and uncles. They all sent me a message, and he wrote it down. Miss Fox read it to me."

"Then you ought to answer it," decided Cora Mae. "And I'm going to write to my family too. Let's ask Miss Fox."

Miss Fox thought letters a wonderful idea, and so did Mrs. Hughes. It became a class project, and everyone was expected to write one. The letter didn't need to include much news. In fact, this was impossible, since the writing class had not progressed so far as that. It was just the idea that families at home wanted to hear how their children were getting along, if they were well and happy, and how they liked the school.

A form was written on the blackboard, so that those who had trouble in thinking of what to say or how to form the words would have something to copy.

Mrs. Hughes was especially pleased with the idea, for the letter-writing project increased their general knowledge and vocabulary as well. They learned about mail and the postal system, about postage stamps, and about how their messages would be carried from Oregon to the reservation. It took a full week of preparation before they started writing, for they had to learn many new words first.

Rose began her letter reluctantly. She wrote the word "Dear," then went down the new list of words they had learned until she came to "Grandmother." There were many words in this list: mother, father, sister, brother, aunt, uncle, and so on. Some of the children were lavishly including them all in the salutation, in order not to slight anyone. She gripped her pencil tightly as she copied the short sentences in the prepared form on the blackboard.

"I am well. I like school. We have good things to eat. I study hard. I wrote this myself."

Laboriously she added her name, "Rose Smith," and wondered if Grandmother, provided she ever received the letter, would know who sent it.

She was the first one through. She put her pencil in the holder and sat with closed hands waiting for the others. Mrs. Hughes came down the aisles, glancing at papers as she walked by. She paused to read Rose's letter and patted her on the shoulder.

"Very good, Rose," she approved. She laid a white envelope on the desk before she went on.

Rose folded her letter carefully, as she had been shown in the earlier demonstration, and slipped it into the envelope. She must wait now for individual help in addressing it. No form written on the blackboard would do for that. Miss Fox noticed that her envelope was waiting and came to the desk.

"For whom is your letter, Rose?" she asked.

"My grandmother."

"Has she an English first name?"

Rose shook her head quickly. Miss Fox would understand that no Navaho name could be used promiscuously on the envelope.

"She would be Mrs. Smith," said Miss Fox thoughtfully, "but that might be confused with others in the family. I think, in this case, 'Grandmother Smith' would be all right on the address."

Rose carefully wrote where Miss Fox showed her.

"You write well, Rose," said Miss Fox. "You are doing well in all your schoolwork. What is the name of the trading post where your grandmother's mail would come?"

Rose told her, and Miss Fox wrote "Goose Hollow, Arizona," on a piece of paper for Rose to copy on the envelope below Grandmother's name.

The last thing was the stamp. Miss Fox passed them out when everyone was finished, and there was great excitement as they were being licked and applied. The letters were finished, the stamps meant that they would be sure to be carried safely, and in a couple of days these little white envelopes would be in the hands of loved ones miles away.

"Now we'll go to the post office," announced Miss Fox unexpectedly, and the room grew very noisy indeed.

They hadn't realized that they were to be allowed to mail the letters themselves. They had supposed that the letters would be collected in class and that someone would post them later on.

"Get on your coats and caps," said Mrs. Hughes carefully. "It is raining."

They hurried to obey, forming their regular marching line of partners. In one place the line widened so that Isobel, Cora Mae, and Rose walked three abreast, but this was an arrangement tactfully ignored by the teachers and accepted without question by the other children. Out into the murky, wet day they marched, but no one noticed the weather. To them it was a splendid day, a day when they were spanning the long miles between themselves and home.

"How long will it take the letter to get there, do you think?" asked Cora Mae softly.

"Two days and two nights. That's what it took us."

"A letter might not take so long. It's not so heavy. I hope they send an answer right away."

"I hope so too. I can hardly wait to get mine."

"What if they don't get it?" asked Rose weakly, and her two friends looked at her in amazement.

"They have to get it," Isobel reminded her. "Don't you remember how Miss Fox told us nothing can interfere with the mails?"

"But what if something does? What if it gets lost? Or maybe the trader forgets to give out the mail? I don't think that very much mail comes to Goose Hollow. I never even knew about mail until I came here."

"He has to give it out," said Cora Mae. "That's the law. He can't keep it."

"Goose Hollow," repeated Isobel thoughtfully. "I've heard of that place. Is that where you live?"

Rose nodded. "And I honestly don't think they have much mail there. What if the trader doesn't know what to do with it?"

"Of course he knows," scoffed Cora Mae. "Didn't Grace Yucca just get a letter from there? And you'll get one, too, just as soon as your family hears from you."

The head of the line turned in at the post office. It occupied one corner of the store, and the interior of the building looked strange to the children as they entered. It was as though they were seeing it for the first time, and certainly the bare counters with the vacant aisles behind them bore little resemblance to Store Hour.

They filed by the slot marked "Outgoing Mail," and one after another white envelopes were relinquished by the brown fingers which held them so tightly. There was still excitement and happiness on each face, but there was an expression of solemnity, too. It was hard to believe that the wheels of the United States mails were rolling for them. The United States mails would carry their letters now, and soon they would be rolling back with a return.

Only Rose did not share in these feelings. Instead she couldn't help thinking that she might just as well have dropped her own letter into a mud puddle outside. Grandmother would never receive it, for no one knew who Grandmother Smith was. And even if she did receive it she wouldn't know how to go about getting an answer to her granddaughter. Rose wondered how long it would be before the people here started asking questions about her.

CHAPTER TWELVE

Christmas came as a complete surprise to Rose. Most of the other students had known something about the holiday, either from missionaries or traders and their wives who had held celebrations for their Navaho customers. Unfortunately, the trader at Goose Hollow had done nothing about Christmas. He was a good man and fair in his dealings with the Indians, but his mind was on his daily business and a Christmas celebration simply did not occur to him.

The significance of the day was explained to the class by Miss Fox and repeated in the instructional period which preceded church. By this time Rose was attending Sunday services regularly with Cora Mae, who had chosen the Protestant group because of early contacts with the Presbyterian Mission close to her home. None of this prepared Rose for Santa Claus, sleigh bells, decorated trees, and gifts.

There had been rumors in the twelve-year-old room of a forthcoming party, for the older children had been talking.

"Will it be like the State Fair?" asked Rose, wondering

if she should write a small check on the school bank in preparation. Fourteen dollars was a lot of money. Perhaps it wouldn't hurt to draw out a quarter in honor of Christmas. "Do we go on the bus?"

"I don't think so," said Isobel. "I think the party will be here. The people will come here."

"Who?"

"The people who give us the party," nodded Cora Mae. "It's a lot of men from Salem. A club, I think. I don't know its name."

"How can they make a party?"

"They'll probably give us candy," said Isobel, remembering the generosity shown at her nearest trading post at Christmas. "Candy makes a party, doesn't it?"

"Yes," agreed Rose quickly. She was glad that she wouldn't have to draw money from the bank. More than anything she wanted to ride on the big wheel that went up in the sky at the State Fair, but if there was no wheel at the party she could save her money.

Even the most experienced first-year students were wide-eyed with astonishment and pleasure when they trooped into the auditorium on Christmas Eve. On the stage was a gigantic fir tree, hung with sparkling tinsel and variegated balls and stars. A thousand lights seemed to twinkle from the branches. The students sat staring in open-mouthed admiration, but even before they had recovered from the surprise a fat little man, dressed in a red suit which was trimmed in fur no whiter than his beard, appeared from the wings to the music of tinkling bells.

He laughed a great deal, did the red-coated man, who said his name was Santa Claus, and because his laughter was infectious the children laughed too, without knowing why. A couple of men appeared, who seemed to be his helpers, and as the children filed by Santa Claus handed out gifts. They were fine gifts, too: silk stockings and scarfs and perfume to the older girls, bright shirts and ties to the older boys. The twelve-year-olds were delighted to discover that when it was their turn to walk before Santa Claus he was giving out toys, baseballs and bats, pocket knives and dolls, games and embroidery kits and paint sets.

After that there were refreshments, not just candy— although there was plenty of that in red net stockings —but also ice cream and cookies and punch.

It was a Christmas that they would remember always, and even after the next day with its special church service and its big dinner of roast turkey and dressing, they were still talking about it.

"We never had anything like this at home," admitted Isobel. "The trader used to have a party on Christmas and everyone was invited. He roasted a sheep, and we all ate all we could hold. Then he gave everybody a bottle of pop, and candy to us children, and we didn't have to pay for anything. But it wasn't like this."

"I should say not," agreed Cora Mae promptly. "At the
Mission they used to have a tree, but it didn't sparkle. It
had chains made of paper, and strings of rose berries. I
can hardly wait to tell my family about this Christmas.
Real presents!"

"I wonder if my family went to the trader's this

year," said Isobel thoughtfully. "I hope they had a Christmas."

"Me too," said Cora Mae. "But they probably had one at the Mission."

Rose had been happily painting with her new drawing set. It was quite the most wonderful set she had ever seen, for not only were there water colors in every imaginable shade, but crayons, books filled with pictures to color, colored paper to make freehand drawings, scissors to cut them out, and paste to stick one paper onto another. It had kept her busy every spare moment, and she could hardly wait to get back to it after lunch; but suddenly it lost its charm.

She was realizing that Grandmother did not know what Christmas was. To Grandmother it was just another day, a day filled with household duties, caring for the sheep, bringing in the wood, melting snow for water, preparing a meal, and trying to keep warm before the smoking fire. It wasn't fair. Everyone else, it seemed, had a happy Christmas. Why should Grandmother have to do without?

Then Rose remembered the wonderful institution called the mails and realized that it was in her own power to make Christmas for Grandmother. What did it matter if it came a little late? Grandmother wasn't expecting it, anyway. She felt warm and excited, and the paint brush in her hand quivered with eagerness, jumping outside of the lines of the picture she was coloring.

"I'm going to ask permission to go to town next Saturday," she announced abruptly. "I'm going to take money from the bank and buy a present."

Trips to town were one of the real treats to the students, especially so for the first-year pupils, since the number they might make during the year was limited. Rose had been there only once and considered the excursion almost as thrilling as the State Fair and second only to the Christmas party in excitement. They had to go with an interpreter, who planned the excursion ahead and escorted groups who as yet did not have sufficient knowledge of English to venture forth alone.

Unfortunately for her plans no group was going to town on the first Saturday following Christmas, and Rose had to wait an extra week. It was frustrating, but somehow she managed to restrain herself. If someone didn't know about Christmas in the first place, an extra week wouldn't make much difference.

On the Friday before the expedition she went to the school bank and carefully made out a check. The boy who was acting as banker looked at it curiously.

"This wipes you out," he reminded her. "You won't have anything left if you draw out this much."

"I know."

He shrugged his shoulders as he counted out fourteen dollars and slid them across the ledge. Then he held out his hand for her checkbook, and she tried to smile as she surrendered it. It wasn't a very strong smile, but it was the best she could manage as she watched the precious checkbook drop into the drawer. She was poor again. She was no longer the respected citizen with money in the bank. She tried to remind herself that the primary purpose of money was to buy what you wanted, and she knew what she wanted to buy.

For the other children in the bus the excitement of the day began the moment they climbed in and the driver threw in his clutch. It was a holiday, and even the cold rain which pounded against the windows could not dampen their spirits. They loved the stop lights which flashed green to red, and marveled that such a little thing as a light had power to regulate a moving vehicle. Rose was only impatient with the delay. Her hand tightly clutched the money in her coat pocket, and her thoughts were far ahead of the bus.

On their arrival in town they went first to the five-and-ten-cent store, and here Miss Fox allowed them to separate. Everyone was permitted to wander and look as he pleased, under promise not to venture outside the building and to gather in a specified corner after a few minutes. At first Rose was excited by this store, too, but a frantic search soon told her it did not contain what she sought. There were tears in her eyes when she confessed the problem to Miss Fox.

"No," agreed Miss Fox hesitantly. "But that is very expensive, Rose. It will take a lot of money. You can't afford it."

The tears seemed to swell, and Miss Fox became only a blurred image before her eyes.

"I will show you," decided Miss Fox after a moment. "It will be a good lesson for all of you in the value of money. We will go to the store which sells it, and the clerk will tell us how much it costs. There will be other things there, just as pretty and much more suitable, and they will not cost nearly so much."

When the children finally collected in the corner Miss Fox led them outside, down the rain-swept street, to another store. This one sold clothing, for the window was filled with large figures of ladies dressed in fur-trimmed coats so lifelike that the children could scarcely believe they were not real people.

Miss Fox led them through a section which displayed handbags and another which must sell stockings, for on the counters there were legs without people attached. Everyone giggled and laughed at these funny-looking legs without people. Finally they came to some tables holding bolts of material. The children recognized these instantly, for every trading post kept bolts of material laid away on the shelves. None so pretty as these, however. Here were shiny satins in every conceivable shade, laces and nets, beautiful prints and stripes and figures. The Navahos were open-mouthed at the splendor.

Miss Fox spoke to a saleslady, then called to Rose.

"She says they are having a sale on velveteens today. But even at sale prices you will see that they are too expensive. A pretty printed cotton or even a lightweight wool will not cost so much. It will be in much better taste for school, too."

As the clerk began putting bolts of rich velveteen on the counter everyone said "Oh!" in admiration. There was black, as rich and deep as a cat's fur. There was a shade of turquoise that put the finest stone to shame, and there was a red. It was a red made of sunsets over the desert and of certain leaves in the fall when Changing Woman is preparing to take on old age. The fire was in it, too, not the flames themselves, but the deep-glowing coals beneath. It was a proud color and a rich one, and it was sure to lend something of its own qualities to its wearer.

Rose's small hand shot out quickly.

"I'll take that one," she decided, and her other hand dug deeply into her pocket for her precious fourteen dollars. Already she had learned that in the white man's world there was no bargaining. One paid the asked price or did without.

"Oh, Rose," began Miss Fox sadly. "Let's look at something else. Something not so expensive will make you just as pretty a dress. This is $2.89 a yard."

"But it is not for me," cried Rose, pulling back in amazement. "It is for my grandmother. I will send it to her through the mail. I will make Christmas."

"Christmas?" repeated Miss Fox, but the other children understood instantly and murmured their approval.

"She has never had one," explained Rose simply. "Her

dress is old and much worn. As long as I can remember she has had only that one. She has never had so fine a one as this. I want to give it to her. When she gets it, it will be Christmas."

Miss Fox seemed to understand then. She looked at Rose's intent face carefully, then she spoke again with the clerk who counted the money Rose had laid on the counter.

"There is not enough for a whole dress," Miss Fox told Rose finally. "But there will be plenty for a blouse of the velvet, and we can buy calico to make a full skirt. Calico is not expensive. You will need thread, and we must save out money for postage. It costs more to mail a package than it does a letter. Are you sure you want to spend it all?"

"Oh yes," Rose cried happily, fingering the glowing velvet on the counter. A velvet blouse was quite enough. Even the richest women in Goose Hollow wore calico skirts, and none of them had blouses of so soft a texture, so warm a color. "When my grandmother receives this she will truly know about Christmas."

CHAPTER THIRTEEN

"We are going to have a birthday party," announced Miss Fox, smiling at the class. "Can you guess whose birthday it is?"

The children looked from one to another eagerly. They knew about birthdays. Records had been kept on the reservation, and birthdays were observed once a week by special treats at dinner. Finally George Yellowjacket raised a cautious hand.

"I will have a birthday in March, Miss Fox," he admitted.

"But this is only February, George," she reminded him. "The birthday we are getting ready to celebrate is in February. Can't anyone guess whose it is?"

Mrs. Hughes wrote two words on the blackboard, and the children's eyes followed the tracings of white chalk carefully. They were hard words but not too unfamiliar, for they had seen them before.

"Chemawa School!" chorused the children, a few of the slower readers coming in late like an echo.

"That's right," nodded Miss Fox. "Every year we celebrate the birthday of Chemawa School. It was born on

February 25, 1880, and is one of the oldest Indian schools in the whole country. Listen carefully and I will tell you the story of our school."

The Navahos folded their hands carefully on their desks and gave the interpreter their attention. They liked stories. It was a little like sitting in the hogans on a winter night, listening to the old ones tell tales of their own people. Some of the oldest still remembered the Long Walk to Fort Sumner, when the Navahos were forced to admit defeat and knew their greatest suffering. There were stories, too, of happier days, when the braves returned laden with rich booty from a raid, and when the land was still rich and the flocks of sheep so large that they dotted the fields like daisies in the springtime. It had never occurred to them that the school itself might have a story to tell, and they were eager to hear it.

Chemawa was not always in this place, Miss Fox told them. It began as a small school for only eighteen Indians in a spot thirty miles from here. It was in connection with a larger school for whites, and the first superintendent was a white lieutenant from the army. So many Indians wanted to come to the school, however, that the space was not large enough, and it was moved to this spot a few years later.

Finally the name of Chemawa was given to it. Chemawa was an Indian name of the Chemeketa tribe, and meant Happy Home. It was happy, too, although its first pupils worked hard to make it so. The boys felled trees and dug out stumps to clear the land upon which the buildings now stood. The girls cooked and sewed and washed for everyone in the school. But no one seemed to mind the hard work. More and more Indian children came to the school.

At first there were only Oregon Indians; then, because it was a government school, tribes from other states in the Northwest began to send their children here too. And that was good, for the tribes became friends with one another and there was no more talk of war or petty quarrels. Then the Indians of the Northwest began to move off the reservations and live in towns with the whites. Their children went to white schools, and only when they were orphans or came from broken homes where there was no family to take care of them did they come to Chemawa as wards of the government.

The Navahos shook their heads sadly as they thought of these poor orphans without families. There were around a hundred and fifty of them here at Chemawa now. They lived in the same dormitories and ate in the same dining rooms, but because their language was English they did not attend classes with the Navahos and had only sign-language communication with the younger group.

Johnny Paul put up his hand, and Miss Fox paused to ask the question which was troubling him.

"But Miss Fox," he said in amazement. "They seem happy, these Northwesterners. I play ball with some of them. They laugh and seem like everyone else."

"Of course they're happy. When your own English is better, so that you can talk with them and hear their thoughts, you will know that they are happy."

Johnny Paul shook his head doubtfully, and Rose concentrated very hard on her folded hands. She felt her cheeks grow warm and hoped that no one would glance in her direction. They might guess her secret. They were feeling sorry now for the Northwesterners at Chemawa without families, but how would they feel if they knew that one of their own class members was almost as badly off?

"And that's where you came in," continued Miss Fox brightly.

At the time when fewer and fewer Indians of other tribes were patronizing government schools, someone in Washington recognized the great need of the Navahos. There were more Navahos than any other tribe and fewer schools where they could go. Why not utilize these vacant classrooms throughout the country for the new Five-Year Navaho Plan? The facilities were there, and it was more economical to take the students to existing schools than to build new ones close at home.

"That's why you're here," concluded Miss Fox. "That's why you have a part in Chemawa's birthday next week. There will be a Navaho girl on the royal court. A Navaho may even be elected queen of the Birthday Ball. And certainly there will be Navaho dances and ceremonies, along

with those of other tribes who have gone to school here. You are a part of Chemawa. It's your school, and the birthday is just as important as you want to make it."

Miss Fox had purposely selected the end of the last period in which to make her announcement, and it was a good thing she did. The prospects of the birthday party, which could be as important as they wanted to make it, drove everything else from their minds.

"Do you suppose we'll get to be in one of the dances?" asked Cora Mae as they started across the campus.

"They'll probably choose the boys," said Rose regretfully. "That's natural."

"Not for the ceremonies," objected Isobel. "She said ceremonies, too."

"Anyway, we'll get to go," said Cora Mae. "And we'll

get some of the birthday cake. If it's big enough. Mrs. Hughes said so."

"Imagine a cake big enough for everybody to have a piece of it," marveled Rose.

"It has to be big. There'll be seventy-six candles on it," said Isobel. She stopped in the path, and her forehead wrinkled with distaste. "I wish I didn't have to go to basketball practice. You'll talk about the birthday party, and I won't know what you say."

"You've got to go," exclaimed Rose in alarm. "You're the only one from our room who made the first-year team. And you're going to play against the second-year girls Friday night."

"That's just because I'm tall," said Isobel modestly. "But don't talk about the birthday, or, if you do, remember everything you say so you can tell me."

Although speculation ran high there were no new developments about the party until the next afternoon when the door of the classroom opened and a group of older girls walked in. Mrs. Hughes stopped the lesson while she went over to greet the newcomers, and the twelve-year-olds sat quietly, their black eyes taking in every detail. The visitors were older students. One was a Navaho, and because she was older she lived in the upper-grade dormitory and attended advanced classes. The twelve-year-olds had never spoken with her, but they knew her name was Betty Sweetwater. The other two girls were Northwesterners.

Mrs. Hughes looked at the class hopefully and said something in English. More and more she was addressing them directly these days, and sometimes they could understand her. Today they were too excited, so Miss Fox had to speak in Navaho.

"These are the three candidates for queen of the Birthday Ball, children," she explained. "This is Amy Ball, the ninth-grade representative. She is of the Klamath tribe. This is Georgia Kiatti from the senior high school. Georgia belongs to the Blackfoot tribe. The third candidate is from the Navaho program, and her name is Betty Sweetwater."

The children clapped loudly and enthusiastically, and the older girls smiled.

"Later on there will be ballot boxes, and you will all have a chance to vote for the girl you would like to be queen," said Miss Fox. "The other two candidates will be princesses in her court, and the one who receives the most votes from the student body will be queen. They have come here today so that you may see them and know for whom you are voting."

Again the class applauded, and now they looked at the three girls in a new light. It was a great responsibility helping to select a queen for the school. A queen must have many virtues. Which of these three had the right ones?

It grew even more confusing as the day of the election approached. Older students who had heretofore ignored the twelve-year-olds or at least treated them with condescension now wanted to help them make up their minds.

"Be sure you vote for Betty Sweetwater," some of them advised.

"Why?" asked Cora Mae. "Do you think she'll make the best queen?"

"Of course she will. Besides, she's our candidate. She's a Navaho."

So loyalty to one's own people should be considered, even though Miss Fox tried to assure them that at Chemawa they were one family.

"You better vote for Georgia Kiatti," an older boy told them an hour later.

"Why?" It was Rose's turn to question now. "Because she's an orphan, and we should feel sorry for her?"

"No. She's the prettiest. And besides, that Betty's kind of stuck-up."

Wherever they went it was the same thing. Each candidate had her own followers, and they were determined to garner as many extra votes as they could.

"It's called electioneering," Miss Fox explained when they told her about it. "You'll find the same thing going on in almost any election. But in a democracy everyone can vote as he chooses. The ballot is secret. No one knows how you vote, and it's up to you to make up your mind which candidate you think will do the best job."

After the ballots were counted Betty was announced as

queen, and when she appeared on the stage of the audi-
orium dressed in white-beaded buckskin with her pretty
attendants just a step behind her, the applause was thun-
derous. Even those who had voted for the others gave
in gracefully and congratulated the winner. The first-year
students, who had been so concerned with their own
responsibility in electing a queen, were pleased with the
choice. Of course, all the girls were beautiful and queenly,
but Betty looked just right for the part.

Now there was more excitement than ever, for the
special day was almost here. The gymnasium was never
empty, for some group was always practicing one of the
dances; and already the decorating committee was at
work, twisting a false ceiling of colored crepe paper. To
their brief disappointment Isobel, Cora Mae, and Rose
had not been chosen for one of the dances. There were
too many Navahos clamoring for that honor. But they
were to have a part in the program, anyway. They were
in the chorus which sang behind the group enacting the
corn-grinding ceremony, and this was important enough.

"I wish we had beautiful buckskin dresses trimmed
with fringe and beads," mourned Cora Mae.

"It won't matter," said Rose, trying to put down her
own yearning for the same thing. "Nobody will look at
us anyway. They'll be looking at the queen and the
dancers."

The Birthday Ball and pageant were held at night.
Although the girls had seen the decorations earlier in the

day everything seemed new and glamorous as they trooped into the gymnasium after supper. There was a big painted backdrop of Mount Hood on the stage, with fir trees scattered around the sides to give the effect of a forest. The lights, shining through the crepe-paper ceiling, cast a rosy light on the polished gymnasium floor. Around the edges were rows of chairs, for many outside guests had been invited.

But what took everyone's eyes immediately and made groups stop short in the doorway until they were pushed on by those behind was the birthday cake. It occupied a place of honor on a lace-spread table just below the stage, and it was so large it covered almost the whole table top. It was baked in graduated tiers and iced in white with scrolls and flowers in the icing. On each of the three high tiers were candles, rows upon rows of candles, waiting to be lighted.

"You see," whispered Cora Mae triumphantly. "It is a big cake. It's big enough for everybody in the world, so we'll get a piece."

They took their places in the row of chairs where they were to sit until it was their turn on the program. It was exciting to be there, to watch the people swarm through the doorway and be seated by the ushers. At last every seat was filled and the lights in the main gymnasium went out, leaving only those on the stage. Mount Hood glittered and sparkled in the background, and the forest of trees with its central clearing looked more natural than ever.

A teacher who had one of the older rooms appeared at the side of the stage and began to speak to the audience. The first-year students could not understand all the words, but they knew she was telling about Chemawa's birthday. Students dressed in costume appeared on the stage at this point, and Rose realized they were re-enacting the beginning of the Indian school. Trees were cleared, classes began, and more and more students arrived.

New groups performed the ancient tribal dances of their own people, the Owl Dance, the Hoop Dance, the Buffalo and the Eagle Dances. Soon it was time for the appearance of the Navahos, and while the boys were dancing the Yahechai Dance from the Nine-Day Ceremonial, Rose and the others who took part in the singing quietly left their seats to stand beside the stage.

She was glad that the gymnasium was in dusky shadows, and it didn't matter now that she had no buckskin dress to wear. If she were in costume someone might look at her, and it was bad enough to have to sing. Her hands were damp with moisture, and she kept her own eyes on the corn grinders on the stage; but somehow she managed to get through the many verses necessary for the ceremony.

After the pageant the candles were lighted and the cake was cut. Students who had had no other part in the program distributed slices to everyone in the audience, as well as to the dancers behind scenes. Rose had been so busy with her own cake that she hardly noticed the changes going on on-stage. When she glanced up she saw that it was newly occupied by musicians, men with horns and violins and drums. As she watched, the leader lifted his baton and all the instruments joined in the fanfare.

"They're going to start the dancing!" whispered Cora Mae in excitement. "We get to dance the Rabbit Dance, and then we get to watch the others. We don't have to go back to the dormitory for a whole hour yet."

The queen and her court appeared below the stage, and behind them came the senior class. The ball would start with the Rabbit Dance, the social dance of the Northwest tribes, after which waltzes and fox trots, rumbas and two-steps would occupy the rest of the evening.

All the students knew the Rabbit Dance. The Navahos, to whom it was foreign, had been carefully coached in the preceding week, and everyone was expected to join in. Rose, Isobel, and Cora Mae had been looking forward to it. They had spent long hours practicing and had hardly been able to wait for this moment. Now as they watched the queen and her escort, followed by the seniors, step forward, they realized with horror there was something wrong. It wasn't as they had imagined it would be.

"They're pairs!" gasped Rose.

"A boy and a girl," echoed Cora Mae. "And the boys are doing the asking."

Couple by couple the juniors were following the seniors onto the dance floor. Soon it would be time for the first-year students to join in the moving lines of dancers.

"There's nobody dancing in threes," whispered Isobel. "And that's how we practiced."

"If nobody asks us we'll just pretend it's a squaw dance. We'll ask them," said Cora Mae fiercely. She leaned forward in the row, looking down the line of first-year students. Then she settled back and announced a little smugly, "Tom Beaver just winked at me. I guess I've got a partner when it's our turn."

"They'll have to ask somebody." Rose tried to console herself as well as Isobel. "Everybody's supposed to dance."

The floor was getting crowded now. Only the row of first-year students remained sitting in the Navaho section. For one agonizing interval Rose thought the boys intended to remain in their seats. Then a few of the braver ones began getting to their feet. She tried not to look at them and appear too anxious.

Out of the corner of her eye she saw Johnny Paul stop before Isobel and heard Isobel's involuntary gasp of relief. Then someone had stopped in front of her. She made herself look up, trying not to show quite how grateful she was not to be the last one chosen.

"I'm not very good at this," confessed Tony Yucca, "but we got to do it, and I'll try not to step on you."

He looked miserable and unhappy, and his eyes were imploring her to help him. He didn't look sorry for her at all, only sorry for himself.

"Oh, that's all right," she said gaily. "It's all right if you do."

CHAPTER FOURTEEN

Replies from their letters home had been coming in for the last three months. One or two of the children received answers within a week or ten days, but most of the others had taken longer. Arrival of the communication was always announced in class by its owner, and everyone marveled anew at the magic of the mails. Only two children, Rose and Danny Two, had as yet received no reply, and the week after the birthday party the thing Rose had been dreading most of all occurred. Danny Two had a letter from his family.

"Yours will come," said Isobel comfortingly. "It's just taking a little longer, that's all."

"Maybe every time someone from your family went to the post the trader was too busy to write a letter for him," consoled Cora Mae. "Traders can get pretty busy sometimes."

"I know," nodded Isobel. "Somebody has to keep going back all the time to be there when he doesn't have much to do. I'm glad my brother learned to write so we don't have to wait for the trader."

"Our trader is pretty busy," said Rose, grateful to both

of them for finding an excuse. "And so is my family. We hardly ever go to the trading post."

"One of them will, though," Isobel assured her quickly. "One of them will be there someday when the trader doesn't have anything to do. Then he'll write an answer to your letter."

Rose knew that it would never happen. She felt that her classmates were wondering about it, perhaps talking among themselves. Was her family so uncaring as to leave her without any letter, or, worse, did she have no family to write a letter? She didn't believe that Grandmother had ever received the letter mailed to Goose Hollow. How could she, when Grandmother didn't even know her new name was Smith? Worst of all, Rose now remembered that the beautiful red velvet had been mailed in the same way. She had been so carried away with the Christmas spirit that she had trustingly sent it to the same address. There had been no acknowledgment, and it was almost more than she could bear to think of that glowing velvet. Perhaps it was still in the mail, being carried from here to there, looking for an owner. Or perhaps there was a Grandmother Smith somewhere other than Goose Hollow, a stranger who was even now preening herself in the luxury of the material.

She thought about it more and more, and before long she could think of nothing else. She lay awake at night thinking of it. It drove everything else from her mind, and her schoolwork began to suffer. Miss Fox talked with her about it, wondering if something was wrong, but Rose assured the teacher-interpreter that she only needed to study harder and that she felt fine.

Every day her face seemed to grow sadder and more thoughtful. She hardly ever laughed, and her smiles were slow in coming, as though she had been thinking of something else and hadn't heard what people were saying. Her appetite was gone, too, and after every meal she had to scrape a good deal of food from her plate before putting it into the pile of dishes to be washed.

"Rose, are you homesick?" Isobel demanded abruptly one noon as the girls were walking toward the cafeteria. She and Cora Mae both looked at her so intently that Rose knew this was no spur-of-the-moment question. They must have been discussing the change which had come over her.

"No," she denied quickly. "And I'll have a letter soon. You'll see."

"You're not worrying because you haven't had an answer to your letter?" exclaimed Cora Mae in surprise. "Do you think that someone at home is sick, just because you haven't heard?"

"It doesn't mean that at all," said Isobel quickly. "Look! There's that girl who comes from the same place as you. Let's ask her if she's heard from her family."

Rose shot a startled glance at the chattering group of girls ahead of them on the walk. One of them was Grace Yucca.

"No, no," she protested, reaching out to pull Isobel back. Isobel, however, was determined. She lifted her voice and called.

"Grace! Grace Yucca! Wait a minute."

The girls heard and turned to see who was trying to attract their attention. Grace must have thought it was Rose, for she smiled at her directly and said hello.

"Ask her," insisted Cora Mae loudly. "Ask her now."

Grace stopped, and a puzzled expression replaced her smile.

"Ask me what?"

"She wants to know if you've heard from your family," said Isobel bravely. It was not too easy to bridge the age gap and start conversation with these older girls. "And if you have, whether they mentioned hers. She wants to know if all of her family are well."

"All of her family?" repeated Grace stupidly. She recovered herself in an instant. "I heard from my family last week. Everything is as usual at home. They had not seen your grandmother recently, but there had been snow and she may not have been able to get out very far. They said the last time they saw her that she was well."

"You see," said Isobel triumphantly.

But Cora Mae was not satisfied. This older girl was friendly and communicative. Perhaps there was more information they could find out for Rose.

"Had they seen any others in Rose's family?"

"No," said Grace after a moment. Her face wore a queer

look. Rose waited for her to explain that there was no one else but Grandmother. Instead Grace turned back to her own group, and they continued on their way.

Rose hardly knew whether to be relieved or not. Grace hadn't given her away this time, but what would she do next? Then there was Tony Yucca. He also knew her secret, and he might blurt it out at any minute. Such news would travel fast. It would be all over school in no time, and everyone would feel sorry for her. It was torture to have it hanging over her head like a promised punishment, not knowing when it would happen. Perhaps it would be better to get it over with.

"Well, at least they saw your grandmother and talked with her," pointed out Isobel. "And if anyone else in the family had been sick or in trouble she would have said so."

"So there's nothing to worry about," said Cora Mae briskly. "Come on. I'm starving."

Rose was unable to choke down any of her meal today. She sat at the table with her friends, wondering how long they would be her friends after the truth finally came to them. Oh, it wasn't that they wouldn't like her, but their liking would be tinged with pity. They would feel that they had to guard their tongues when they were around her. They would feel that they must avoid any reference to their own families, lest she feel her lack of one. It would grow harder to do. Their relations would be strained, and before long they might even avoid her. It wasn't pleasant to be around people who made one feel sad.

She dragged through her afternoon classes, hardly knowing what was going on. The evening meal was even worse than at noon. Food seemed to swell up in her mouth, and it was difficult to swallow. Most of it remained untouched on her plate.

The next morning she was too tired to get up. Isobel and the twins called her several times, and when they were finally convinced that something was the matter Maria ran to fetch the matron.

"I don't believe she has a fever," Mrs. Masters told the older girl who accompanied her as interpreter. "But I do think the infirmary is the best place for her until we see what develops. Ask if she is able to walk, will you?"

Rose sat up in bed when she was told to. Everything was strange, as though she were far away and this was happening to someone else. It must be someone else sitting on the edge of the bed holding out one foot after the other so that the scuffs she had made in home economics could be slipped on. She herself seemed to be sitting off in the distance watching, while this strange, detached person whom the matron and the older girl called Rose obeyed their commands.

Because they weren't sure what was the matter with her they put her to bed in a room by herself. The nurse took her temperature and confirmed Mrs. Masters's opinion that there was no fever. Everyone seemed pleased about that except Rose, who didn't care. Nothing mattered any more.

When the doctor came to examine her she answered his questions through an interpreter, hardly knowing what they were. No, she didn't hurt. She had no pain. She was only tired, so tired she could hardly lift her arm. No, she wasn't hungry. She wanted nothing but to be left alone.

"Do you want to go home and have a Sing?" asked the interpreter finally. "Do you think a Sing would make you well again?"

"No," said Rose weakly. "No Sing."

She saw the look of surprise exchanged by the doctor and the nurse at her reply. Perhaps they had thought she was only feigning this tired feeling or that she had no faith in their medicines. Any Navaho too ill to care about his Sing is very ill indeed.

They went away, leaving her alone, and she drifted into a dreamless sleep.

The next day Miss Fox came to see her. Rose had been awake for some time, lying quietly staring at the white ceiling. Miss Fox crossed the room and stood looking down on her. Rose stared back, wondering if Miss Fox knew, if Isobel and Cora Mae had told her. Perhaps, though, it had taken them longer than she thought to read the pitying expression on Grace Yucca's face. Perhaps even yet they had not guessed that she had no family. She decided that Miss Fox was still unaware of the secret, for although in her eyes was distress there was no pity in them.

"How do you feel, Rose?"

"I'm tired."

"I know. This has been coming on for a long time. I knew something was wrong and so did your friends. Can I do anything for you?"

"No, Miss Fox."

Miss Fox bit her lip and looked worried.

"The doctors can't decide what it is," she said finally. "Do you have any ideas, Rose?"

"No, Miss Fox."

"Your friends are anxious about you. Isobel and Cora Mae want to come and see you just as soon as it's permitted. Would you like to see them?"

"No, thank you, Miss Fox." It was an effort to speak. "I—I'd better not."

"There's another girl, too," continued Miss Fox hesitantly. She seemed to be having trouble thinking of things to say. "She was just outside the infirmary door as I came in. I can't remember her name, but she called you Little Sister——"

"Lucy! Lucy Smith!" said Rose. Her eyes seemed to brighten, and her hand which had been lying listlessly in Miss Fox's gave a little jump. "Please let me see her."

"I'll see what I can do," said Miss Fox in surprise. "She may have already gone away. Do you like her very much, Rose?"

"She is my sister," nodded Rose.

Lucy Smith was still waiting in the corridor, and Miss Fox brought her into the room after only a moment's delay. Lucy looked a little awed by the strange surroundings; otherwise her round face was as friendly and good-natured as ever. She came and stood by the bed.

"How do you feel, Little Sister?" she asked hesitantly.

"You see," said Rose, her voice a little stronger. "You see, Miss Fox. This is my elder sister. She is Lucy Smith. I am Rose Smith. We are sisters. Isn't that so, Lucy?"

"Of course," said Lucy. "And you will be well soon. The medicine they give you will make you well."

"I am better already, Elder Sister. The sight of my sister

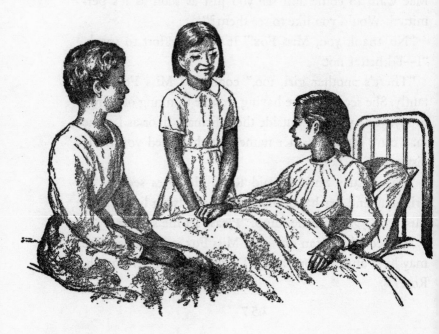

makes me feel much better," answered Rose, looking at Miss Fox to make sure she understood. Perhaps Miss Fox would tell everyone that Rose's sister had visited her and that the sight of a member of the family had improved her health. Miss Fox was a teacher, and her words carried more weight than those of Grace and Tony Yucca.

"I am glad to hear that," said Miss Fox. Suddenly she began to smile. She no longer looked alarmed, only happy that the sisters were reunited and that Rose was feeling stronger. "Would you like me to tell the class that you are better, Rose? Would you like me to tell them that the moment your sister came to see you the sight of her made you feel much better?"

"Yes, please. Tell them that the sight of her is much better than getting a letter from home."

"I'll do that," agreed Miss Fox. She turned to Lucy. "You must go now, Lucy. I hope you'll come again, but we mustn't tire your little sister with too long a visit the first time."

CHAPTER FIFTEEN

By the next day Rose really was better. Even the doctor
said so, although he privately admitted to the nurse that
he had found little wrong in the first place.

"Of course, she's too thin and she seems to be run-
down," he said. "But outside of that there wasn't anything
I could put my finger on. It seemed to be mental, as
though she had decided the battle was a little too hard
for her."

"It couldn't have been that, since she didn't want to go
home and have a ceremonial," the nurse reminded him.
"But her attitude does seem changed. I don't know what
caused it, but for the first time today she spoke of her
classwork and hoped she hadn't fallen so far behind that
she couldn't catch up."

"Don't let her get to thinking that," warned the doctor
quickly. "We don't want her worrying about anything
while she's convalescing. See if you can't get the interpreter from her room to come in and give her a little help as
soon as she's strong enough to take it."

Even Rose agreed that it was better to stay in the infirmary a little longer and rebuild her strength. The weeks

when she had scarcely touched her meals and had lain awake nights when she should have been sleeping had taken their toll. She tired easily, and she couldn't seem to get enough sleep.

She was sitting in a chair by the window one afternoon when the door opened to admit a visitor. It was Store Hour, so she hadn't expected company at all. When she saw it was Grace Yucca some of the old fear and distrust returned to her.

"Hello, Rose," said Grace diffidently.

"Hello." She looked at her visitor carefully, expecting to see the familiar pity she always read into the eyes of everyone at home. To her surprise she saw only embarrassment.

"I brought you some fudge," said Grace, holding out a parcel wrapped in waxed paper. "We made it in home ec today, and I saved some for you."

Rose took the fudge cautiously, wondering if it was charity, like the dress Grace had given her when they left home or the mutton Mrs. Yucca always sent to Grandmother when they killed a sheep.

"I would have come to see you sooner, but I had no gift," explained Grace quickly. "Our teacher told us that it is customary to take little presents when you visit someone who is sick in the hospital. Flowers, usually, but it's too early for them. That's why I waited till we made fudge."

So it wasn't charity after all. It was custom. Isobel, Cora

Mae, and Lucy never brought gifts, but they were younger. They hadn't come upon that point of etiquette in their schoolwork. When she brought the day's class assignment Miss Fox sometimes had a little present, a magazine filled with bright pictures or a colored puzzle for Rose to put together. She smiled and bit into a piece of candy.

"I'm going to write to my family today," said Grace, speaking rapidly. She had picked up the magazine Miss Fox had left and was turning the pages so that she need not look at Rose. "I wondered if there was a message you would like me to write down, so they could give it to your grandmother."

"No." The candy was now tasteless in her mouth. "I can't think of one."

"Mary would be glad to go over to her hogan," continued Grace doggedly. "Or my mother. They like your grandmother very much. They are keeping an eye on her this winter. They say that she is a fine woman and that you are a great credit to her. I hope you are not worrying about her while you are away, because I know they will take care of her."

"I am glad," said Rose.

"Before we left home my mother talked with my brother and me. She said that when we came to the school we must tell no one that only you and your grandmother remain in your family." Grace's cheeks were growing dark with embarrassment. It would have been easier to keep this family discussion to herself, but Miss Fox had convinced her she must confide in Rose. "My mother said that here in a strange place people who do not know your grandmother might not realize what a fine woman she is. They might feel sorry for you, that you have only one in your family. So Tony and I will never tell."

Rose, too, was embarrassed at this frankness, but she was also relieved that her secret was safe. Then the full significance of Grace's remarks came to her.

"But at home everyone feels sorry."

"We feel sorry," admitted Grace reluctantly. "But we admire you. We admire your grandmother for what she has done, and we admire you, too. My father has often said that if an accident should befall your grandmother he would hurry to your hogan so that he might be first to adopt you. He would have to go fast, because he is not the only one in Goose Hollow who would welcome you as a daughter."

"Oh," said Rose in amazement.

Grace stood up quickly, glad that her mission was at an end. Everything she had said was true, but it had been hard to put into words. For the first time since her arrival she smiled at Rose easily, secure in the knowledge that these things would never have to be mentioned again.

"Good-by," she said brightly. "I am glad you are better. I will come to see you again if I can think of another gift to give a sick person."

Rose sat quietly after she had gone, her mind going over

and over the things Grace had said. Was it really true? Could people feel admiration and pity at the same time? Could the emotions be so divided that one would over-shadow the other? In any event she was safe here at school. Tony and Grace would never tell.

Miss Fox came to see her that evening. This time she had no small gift. She pulled a chair up close to the bed, sat down, and drew a yellow paper from her pocket.

"I have something for you, Rose."

Rose looked at the yellow paper inquiringly, and Miss Fox waved it gayly and nodded.

"This is a wire. A telegram," she explained. "They are something like letters, but instead of going through the mail they go through the air. Cora Mae and Isobel thought you might be worried because your grandmother has not answered your letter, so I sent a wire to the trader and he sent one back. Shall I read it?"

"Yes, please," whispered Rose fearfully.

" 'Letter and package received. Grandmother proud as punch. Good health. Fred Johnson, trader.' "

Miss Fox read the telegram aloud, then handed it to Rose, who turned it over and over in her hands. This was from Grandmother. At least it was from the trader at Goose Hollow and indirectly it was from Grandmother. She could announce it when she returned to class. Rose's letter and package had got there. Somehow they had known that She-Who-Knows-Much-Trouble and Grand-mother Smith were the same person. She wondered if

Grandmother had sewed up the new dress and was already wearing it. Rose could imagine her running over to the Yuccas' to display the fine gift. There was no question but that everyone would admire her now.

"That makes you happy, doesn't it?" asked Miss Fox, watching her face. "It is always good to have news from one's family."

"Yes."

"And you are one of the lucky ones, you know," continued Miss Fox. "You have such a large family."

Miss Fox was saying words which did not mean anything. Somehow she must have got the wrong impression. Perhaps she thought all the Smiths in the world were related, and even Rose knew that wasn't so. She and Lucy were not the only ones at school with that name. Possibly this knowledge had somehow escaped Miss Fox.

Miss Fox was her friend, and it was not right to deceive a friend. Rose took a deep breath.

"Miss Fox, I have only a grandmother. She is the only family I have. Lucy is not related to me. I should not have tried to make you think she was."

"But I didn't think so," said Miss Fox quietly. "I knew there was no blood relationship. Your card is here, you know, with your record from the enrollment center. I knew that you and your grandmother were alone. So do the teachers and everyone in the office who has access to those cards."

"You knew it all the time? You have been feeling sorry for me ever since I came?"

"Not at all," denied Miss Fox practically. "Why should I or anyone else feel sorry for you? There is nothing to make me feel sorry. You have good health ordinarily. You are a nice-looking girl, and I need not feel sorry for your looks. You are exceptionally bright and can learn, so I do not need to feel sorry for your lack of brains. You are industrious and have many friends. These are not things to be sorry about."

Rose hung her head in embarrassment.

"The family has always been important to our people," continued Miss Fox seriously. "And since you have come here you are part of a very large one. The Chemawa family. There are six hundred and fifty members of that family here now, and every year more will come. There are members of the Chemawa family who have been graduated and have gone away from here. But there are still ties which bind them to us. Not all of them are Navahos. You remember our birthday pageant and the dances of the other tribes who have gone to school here. They are of your family too. Years from now, if you should meet one of them and discover you were both from this school, you would feel a special bond of kinship."

Rose made herself look at Miss Fox. The teacher-interpreter was very serious. She meant everything she was saying.

"You must never feel that you are alone, Rose. You have a family. A ready-made family which gets larger each year. Some of them will live on the reservation. Others will find work outside, but wherever they are they will have a feeling of loyalty toward Chemawa School and a special feeling of brotherly affection for the members of its family."

"Do you feel that way about Chemawa School, Miss Fox?"

"Yes. That is because I teach here. The boys and girls who go here, especially those in my room, belong to me.

They are my closest family. But I am even luckier than that, for I have another family too—the school at Shiprock where I was a student. I am of that family also, Rose. It will always be very dear to me, even though I don't know the boys and girls who go there now."

"Two families!" said Rose in amazement. She had never seen the school at Shiprock, but she imagined it to be much the same as this one.

For some unexplained reason her mind returned to that first day at Chemawa when the new students had attended assembly. She remembered the words of the white lady who explained the Navaho Five-Year Plan.

"Before you leave, each of you will select some trade, some work that you would like to do. We will train you to do that work."

At the time she had not been able to think of anything she would like to do, outside of returning home and living with Grandmother in the hogan. Now she knew. She would be a teacher-interpreter like Miss Fox. She would have a close family of boys and girls who belonged to her in her room. She would have a larger family, not so close but also dear to her, in the other students. Perhaps like Miss Fox she would teach in a distant school; then she would have two families!

"Miss Fox! Can I do that? Can I be a teacher like you when I finish here?"

Miss Fox smiled. Then she looked thoughtful, as though she were weighing the possibilities of such a thing.

"Yes, Rose," she decided after a moment. "I think you could. It means that you'll have to work hard, harder than anyone in the class. You'll have to finish the work here in less than five years so that you can go into regular school with boys and girls who have been at it since they were six. You won't have to start in the first grade with them, but you will be older than the others in your class and few if any will be of our people. They will not be Navahos. Would you mind that?"

Rose looked at her in amazement. In the few minutes since they had been talking she seemed to have gained new strength. She felt strong enough to do anything, to conquer any problem. Her eyes shone with purpose.

"Oh, Miss Fox," she said reproachfully. "Why should I mind that they are younger and not Navaho? They will still be my family, won't they?"

CHAPTER SIXTEEN

"That's very good, Rose. You iron beautifully," said Mrs. Hughes. She spoke in English, and automatically she looked into Rose's face to make sure she was understood.

"Thank you," answered Rose, speaking carefully so that each word would stand out and not be slurred together. "I like to iron."

Mrs. Hughes nodded and smiled. She picked up her purse from the table and carefully counted out fifty cents. She was glad that she had agreed with Miss Fox's suggestion that her weekly job of ironing be given to Rose instead of to one of the older girls.

"They can speak enough English so they can get along in outside homes for Saturday jobs," Miss Fox reminded her. "Rose can't, and besides she's too young for an ordinary job. But she's quick and wants to learn. She could work for you here on the campus an hour or so after school when you need her. It will give her a chance to learn a little more English if I'm not here to interpret, and besides she needs the money. I'm sure you'll be pleased with her."

Mrs. Hughes was pleased. She was pleased with the way

Rose did the household chores assigned to her and gratified that the girl's understanding of the English language seemed to grow a little more each time she came. Of course, some of this progress might be due to the fact that Rose was now taking her geography period in the second-grade room where more English was spoken. Because she completed her own work before anyone else was finished the geography class had been assigned as extra work to occupy her time.

"Next week?" asked Rose carefully, putting away the iron.

"Next week," nodded Mrs. Hughes. "You come again next week. More ironing."

Rose stepped outside into the late afternoon sunshine. It was the middle of May, and the school year was almost at an end. A lilac bush beside Mrs. Hughes's front walk was in fragrant bloom, and the peonies next to the porch were swollen red buds, threatening to burst at any moment. Almost overnight the grass had grown six inches, and from two different points on the campus she could hear the sound of lawn mowers. Many of the Navahos had been as appalled at the waste of fresh grass as they had at the extravagant use of water. Imagine cutting the top from grass and throwing it away when it could have been used as food for livestock!

The campus was dotted with bright splotches of color where groups of students collected to talk in the few minutes remaining before supper. They sat on the dormitory steps or wandered up and down the walks. The tennis courts and ball field were both in operation, and lines of spectators filled the benches beside each one.

It was a splendid day, one of Changing Woman's best, for she had renewed her youth and everything about her was gay and hopeful and reassuring.

Rose crossed the railroad tracks and followed the winding path to McBride Hall. She spoke to the students sunning themselves on the steps but continued on inside. She had gone straight from her class to Mrs. Hughes's home, and there was barely time to wash before supper. Moreover, she must be especially neat and tidy tonight, for it was the turn of the twelve-year-old room to sit at the Special Table in the cafeteria.

She went to the washroom first, and found Isobel and Cora Mae waiting for her in her own room when she arrived. Both were scrubbed and shining for the Special Table, and Isobel was wearing her turquoise necklace and earrings.

"Hurry up," ordered Cora Mae as soon as Rose arrived. "The sun is nearly down. You haven't much time to comb your hair."

"You know," said Isobel thoughtfully, "the older girls pay no attention to whether it is sundown or not. They comb their hair at night. Lots of times. I've seen them."

"And nothing happens to them?" cried Cora Mae in amazement.

"Nothing. Perhaps that rule of our people does not

mean anything away from the reservation."

"Perhaps it doesn't mean anything at all," said Rose softly. "Perhaps it is one of those things called superstitions that Miss Fox told us about. You know how funny we thought it was that some white people are afraid to walk under a ladder, and if they spill salt they think they must throw some over their shoulders. They believe that such things bring bad luck."

"Combing the hair at night is different," pointed out Cora Mae. "Everyone knows that brings bad luck."

"But maybe not with a comb like this," argued Isobel. "This is not like the combs used by our people in the olden times. The comb may make the difference, and that is why the older girls do not have bad luck."

"Anyway, the sun is not yet down," Rose reminded Cora Mae tolerantly. "I will have time to comb and re-braid my hair if I hurry. You both look very nice," she added, giving them each an approving glance.

Cora Mae smoothed down her new dress proudly. She had made it herself in sewing. Isobel's dress was new, too, and of a daffodil yellow which contrasted with her turquoise jewelry.

"You forgot to put on your bracelet," said Rose, running the comb through her loosened hair, then separating the strands for a fresh braid.

"I decided not to wear it," Isobel shrugged. "This is enough jewelry. Don't you think so?"

"I guess so," agreed Rose. "But the bracelet is beautiful." Suddenly she smiled mischievously and spoke in English. "How was Store Hour?"

Both Isobel and Cora Mae frowned.

"We are not in class," Isobel reminded her. "Speak in our own tongue."

"I should think you'd like to practice." Rose slipped a rubber band on the end of the first braid and began on the second. "The more you speak in English, the quicker you will learn. I asked you about Store Hour."

Cora Mae and Isobel exchanged quick glances.

"The same as usual," shrugged Isobel. "We did not buy anything. We only talked to people."

"I am getting tired of Store Hour," admitted Cora Mae. "It's always the same."

Rose nodded absently. She was ready for supper and just in time, too, for the bell sounded as she was fastening the last button on her fresh dress.

"Come on," cried Cora Mae in excitement. "We mustn't be late. Remember, we're hostesses at the Special Table."

The Special Table was at one end of the long cafeteria, shielded from the rest of the room by screens so that it had a certain amount of privacy. It was occupied almost every night by some group, and this was not the first time the twelve-year-olds had eaten there.

It was arranged by one of the home economics classes, who used it as practice in table setting. There was a white cloth with flowers in the center, and instead of the aluminum plates in everyday use by the rest of the cafeteria there was real china with a painted design, silver laid out at each place beforehand, water in the glasses. The meal was served family style, so that the young Navahos who had first eaten from a common bowl, then stood in line to be served, would learn how to pass things properly.

At the Special Table, too, there were invited guests, usually favorite teachers, and each member of the group occupying the table was a host. He realized his responsibility as such and his duty in carrying on polite table conversation. To sit at the Special Table was a great treat, but it was also very serious. An error by anyone would be a reflection on the whole class.

To everyone's relief and satisfaction the meal went off smoothly. Everyone remembered to unfold his napkin and to cut small bites with his knife. No one spoke with food in his mouth, and when platters and bowls were passed no one heaped his own plate to overflowing. Table conversation was carried on with only a minimum of strain. As the remains of the main course were carried from the table the group beamed at each other proudly.

The girls who were serving at the Special Table now appeared with large trays of frosted cakes. On the top of one of these a candle burned cheerfully, and, seeing it, Rose remembered that this was Birthday Night. Once a week everyone who had celebrated a birthday during the past seven days was honored by a blazing candle on his cake. Usually a birthday was previously discussed a great deal, but no one in the twelve-year-old room had mentioned such a thing. The children looked from one to the other in surprise.

The girl with the tray smiled widely as she walked down the length of the table and stopped beside Rose.

"Happy birthday," she said, and the table hummed with comments and questions.

Rose! It's her birthday! Why didn't you tell us? Why didn't you say something? Were you keeping it a secret?

"But it isn't my birthday!" stammered Rose in amazement. "I don't know when my birthday is. No one ever told me."

As usual when she needed an explanation, she looked toward Miss Fox.

"It's your birthday," agreed Miss Fox. "Maybe you and your grandmother had forgotten the date, but the reservation records haven't. The date of your birth is there on your card. Happy birthday, Rose."

That record card, she thought in amazement. Why, it knew everything there was to know about her. It told things that she didn't even know herself.

Then they began to sing. At almost every table throughout the cafeteria there was a cake with a lighted candle. The students sang the happy-birthday song to the one nearest them, and those at the Special Table sang to her.

"Happy birthday, dear Rose, happy birthday to you!"

She looked up and down the table, at the smiling, friendly faces. Only a few short months ago she had thought them strange and had wondered if she would ever get used to them. Now she was not only used to them, she loved them every one. They meant something very dear to her, and she could read their affection for her in their eyes. Miss Fox was right. They had become her family. Chemawa was well named. It was indeed a happy home.

"Blow out your candle," called someone as the song ended. "Blow it out before it burns into the icing."

"And make a wish," reminded someone else.

There was no need to think of a wish. She had one ready, and she had wished it many times since that day she and Miss Fox had talked together. It was that Grandmother, who was too old for school, could have a family also. She thought it once more, then blew, just as the candle was flickering against the soft icing.

As rapidly as party manners permitted, the iced cakes disappeared around the table. Only Rose's remained intact

in its paper baking cup, the candlewick protruding from a tiny bit of wax. From the head of the table Mrs. Hughes looked down at her questioningly.

"Aren't you going to eat your cake, Rose?"

"No, please. I save it," she said shyly.

It was too hard to put into words, especially into strange English words, what that little cake symbolized to her. It meant her first birthday, the first time she had been singled out for a celebration. She could not count the Yuccas' Blessing Way, planned originally for Grace and Tony. Other people had individual celebrations, but until now it had never happened to her. She couldn't eat the cake, for then the occasion would be only a memory. So long as the cake remained, no matter how hard and dry it became, she would have something to look at which would remind her of this moment.

"Very well then," agreed Mrs. Hughes. She looked around the table, smiling as she placed her napkin beside her plate and pushed back her chair. Instantly napkins appeared from the seclusion of laps where they had been spread. Chairs were pushed back, almost in unison, and the children got to their feet. The Special Table was almost over. Now all that remained was to acknowledge the thank-yous of their guests. This was important, because sometime they might be guests themselves and they must know how to say their appreciation.

One by one the teachers made their rounds and left, and the children, too, were free to go.

"Isn't it wonderful not to have to scrape your own plate and put it in the stack to be washed?" asked Cora Mae as they started for the door.

"Or wash them, either," nodded Rose, remembering one of the extra chores they had all assumed at various times to earn additional clothing. "Where's Isobel? Isn't she coming with us?"

"She went ahead. I saw her walking out with Miss Fox."

"Oh," said Rose in surprise. It wasn't like Isobel to walk away and leave her friends. Perhaps, though, there was some classwork she wanted to discuss with the teacher-interpreter, and she planned to join them later.

The sun was down as they came out of the cafeteria, but there would still be an hour or so of daylight, and no one seemed in a hurry to go inside. No one, that is, except Cora Mae, who insisted on urging Rose on.

"Let's go watch them play ball," suggested Rose, pulling back.

"No, no. It's too cold."

"It isn't cold at all. It's spring."

"I want something from the dormitory. Come with me."

There was no use arguing with Cora Mae once she made up her mind to a thing. Rose gave in good-naturedly, even to following inside the dormitory when she would have much preferred to wait outside on the steps.

To her surprise Cora Mae did not stop at her own door.

Instead she went on down the corridor and paused before Rose's room.

"Well," she said, grinning broadly. "Go on in."

Rose opened the door. Miss Fox was sitting in the chair by the open window, while Isobel occupied her favorite seat on the lower bunk.

"Here comes the birthday girl," said Miss Fox.

"I thought you'd never get here," cried Isobel. "Come on in. There are more surprises."

CHAPTER SEVENTEEN

"More surprises?" repeated Rose. Cora Mae pushed her into the room and closed the door behind them.

"Here," beamed Isobel, holding out a small ribbon-tied package. It was wrapped in some of the red-and-green paper from her own Christmas present which had been carefully saved and laid away in the dresser drawer. "This is for you from me. Happy birthday."

The contents of the package felt bumpy in her hand. Rose untied the bow carefully and unfolded the gay Santa Claus paper.

"Why, Isobel," she gasped in amazement. "It's your turquoise bracelet."

"Not mine," denied Isobel vigorously. "It's yours. I give it to you for a happy birthday."

Rose slipped the bracelet on her arm. It was of heavy silver set with stones graduated from small in the back to large in the front. They were matched in shade and all of the clear greenish blue which said to any Navaho that they were female turquoise. Had they been stones of deep blue with no greenish tinge they would have been male turquoise.

"It's beautiful," she said softly, admiring the glowing color against her brown arm. She had never worn any jewelry. Grandmother had sold hers so long ago that Rose could not remember. She had always wondered how it would feel to wear such luxury, and now she knew.

"But I can't take it, Isobel," she decided reluctantly. "It is too much to give. Too large a present. Your family would not approve."

"They won't care," Isobel assured her earnestly. "When they know how kind you were to me they would want me to give you my bracelet. My mother and her sisters have much jewelry. They wear it every day."

Cora Mae was greatly impressed. While her own family owned some jewelry it was usually in pawn with the trader.

"And your father too? Is he also rich?" she asked curiously. There was no community property between Navaho husband and wife.

"Once he was very poor," said Isobel. "But that was when he was a young man and before he came to Utah. He was a cowboy and broke horses for white men, and little by little he came to own horses of his own. Now he owns many horses. My mother says he has too many, but that is just her way. She is proud, for white men come to buy them of my father and pay much money for them. My father would want you to have the bracelet too."

"I think you should keep it, Rose," said Miss Fox. "It makes Isobel happy to see you wear it."

"Then I will. And thank you, Isobel. Thank you very much." She patted the cool stones that encircled her arm. She could never take it off! Never! And how proud Grandmother would be to see such a display of riches in the family.

"This is my birthday gift," said Miss Fox. She held out what appeared to be an oblong box, wrapped in white and tied with pink ribbon. Cora Mae and Isobel leaned forward, their eyes glistening with excitement.

Rose took the package and unwrapped it carefully. It was a book with a red cover, and when she opened it there were only a few scattered pictures, interspersed with fine printing.

"You aren't ready for it yet," explained Miss Fox, ignoring the looks of disappointment which had appeared on the faces of Cora Mae and Isobel. "But at the rate you're going it won't be long until you are. It's called a dictionary. All the words in the English language are listed there, and after them are written their meanings."

"All the words?" exclaimed Rose in delight. "You mean that as soon as I have learned all the words in this book I will be able to speak English?"

"Much sooner than that," Miss Fox told her. "People who have spoken English all their lives still have to look up words they don't know in the dictionary. If you're going to be a teacher that will be an important book to you someday."

"It is now," Rose insisted. "And I'll start learning the

words right away. Thank you, Miss Fox, for the nice birthday gift."

"And now for mine," interrupted Cora Mae, bouncing up and down on the bunk beside Isobel. "But first I have to tell you about it, and when you know what it is you'll think it's the best one of all."

Rose smiled with bewildered happiness. She could hardly believe all this was happening to her. It must be happening to someone else. A birthday of her own when she never expected to have one, a cake with a candle, and presents from her friends. It seemed too good to be true.

"I felt bad," began Cora Mae, determined to give her own gift a proper build-up, "because I had no birthday gift for you. I had no money in the bank to buy one, either, for I have drawn it out little by little and spent it at Store Hour. I had nothing of my own which would make a good present, as Isobel had.

"We went to Store Hour this afternoon while you were working for Mrs. Hughes. We told you it was the same as always, but it was not quite the same. We went to the post office, as we always do, to ask for any mail. I had no letter, but I did not expect one. Then, because you were not there, I asked if you had a letter. And you did! It is postmarked Goose Hollow, and I brought it to you. It is my gift. Happy birthday."

"A letter? For me?" Rose snatched the envelope from Cora Mae's hands, and her face grew fearful. "Is it bad news? Do you think my grandmother——"

"I hardly think so," said Miss Fox, reaching for the envelope. "It's more likely to be good. If it were bad I think the trader would have notified me. Especially after the wire I sent him when you were ill."

"Then will you read it, Miss Fox?"

"That's what I'm here for. That's why I came, so that once you had the letter you wouldn't have to wait to hear what it says. Unless you want to try to read it yourself, Rose? Perhaps you could."

"Oh no. You, please. It would take me too long."

Miss Fox slit the envelope and drew out the single sheet of paper.

" 'Dear Rose,' " she read aloud. " 'The trader is writing this for me, because your grandmother does not want to have anything to do with letters. I am your uncle——' " She stopped short and looked at Rose in surprise. "I did not know you had an uncle."

"I did once," explained Rose. "My grandmother had a son. He went away. It was a long time ago. Before I was born. I have never seen him and we did not know where he was."

"Apparently he's come home now," nodded Miss Fox. "Or he wouldn't be having the trader write you a letter."

"Oh, Rose, how wonderful!" exclaimed Cora Mae. "How nice to have an uncle come home after a long absence."

"My father always said he would go home sometime and see his own family," remembered Isobel. "I hope he

will take me when he does. It would be fun to see people you have never seen who are really part of your family."

Rose was breathless with excitement. Perhaps the uncle would stay. Perhaps he was married and had brought his wife and children, although that was unlikely, since Navaho men usually lived with their wives' people. However, that did not matter. Now there were three of them in the family. Three was ever so much better than two.

"Do you want me to go on?" asked Miss Fox.

"Yes, please."

" 'I am your uncle. I left this country before you were born,' " continued Miss Fox. " 'I have been away long, but

I have often thought of my mother and my sisters and thought to return for a visit. Now I make that visit. I am sad that my sisters and their husbands are gone. I am sad to find my mother poor and grown old. I am happy to hear of you and welcome you as a niece——' "

"I'm glad he's going to like you," said Cora Mae. "I have an uncle who doesn't like anybody, and nobody likes him."

"Of course he'll like her," insisted Isobel indignantly. "What an idea."

" 'I will wait here with my mother until you arrive,' " went on Miss Fox, her lifted eyebrows warning them to be silent. " 'Then the three of us will go to my new home where I may take care of you. I cannot live here, for my family awaits my return. Your uncle, Many Horse Charley.' "

"Oh!" cried Rose, her excitement bubbling over. "Isobel, Cora Mae, did you hear? Miss Fox, do you know what that means? I have another family! I have the school family, but I have another besides. My uncle speaks of his own family. They will be mine too. When Grandmother and I go to live with him there will be many of us. Oh, I hope it's a big family. I hope he has lots and lots of children."

"He hasn't," said Isobel in a strange voice. "He has only two. But he has sisters-in-law and their husbands and many cousins."

They stared at her in amazement, and suddenly she began to laugh.

"Oh, Rose," she exclaimed as soon as she could stop laughing. "Don't you see? Oh, it's too good to be true. Many Horse Charley is my father! You're my cousin. You're coming home to live with us, forever and ever!"

Rose felt her knees begin to wobble. They were as they had been those first days in the infirmary, too weak to hold her up. She sat down where she stood, in the middle of the floor. She looked at the faces of her three friends, happy and excited at this surprising turn of events.

She tried to speak, but her heart was too full to let words come to her mouth. Then she felt something soft and sticky in her hand and realized that in her excitement she had been squeezing the little cake. It was almost unrecognizable, but the pressure had forced a little more of the candle out of the icing. She straightened it carefully, trying to coax the bedraggled pastry back into shape.

How glad she was that she had kept it. It was a wonderful cake with a magic candle. It had brought fulfillment of her birthday wish. Now Grandmother had a family too.